"I'm trying to think of a way to talk Reece Henderson into reading the script for me.

"He's got just the voice I want, all smooth rawhide and rough velvet," Sydney said.

The camera operator snorted. "If I wasn't married, I'd surely to goodness be trying to get Reece Henderson to do more than *read* to me."

"He's not interested in anything more," Sydney replied, eyes downcast. "I offered to buy him dinner. He turned me down flat."

"Turned you down? Uh-oh. That means he's either A, engaged, B, married, C, gay, or D, in love with his grandmother."

Sydney was forced to fess up. "According to him, it's not A or B, and from the kiss he laid on me the other night, I know it's not C. I can't speak to D, though—"

"For the record," the rawhide-and-velvet voice drawled from the door, "it's E…none of the above."

Dear Reader,

It's summertime. The mercury's rising, and so is the excitement level here at Silhouette Intimate Moments. Whatever you're looking for—a family story, suspense and intrigue, or love with a ranchin' man—we've got it for you in our lineup this month.

Beverly Barton starts things off with another installment in her fabulous miniseries THE PROTECTORS. *Keeping Annie Safe* will *not* cool you off, I'm afraid! Merline Lovelace is back with *A Man of His Word,* part of her MEN OF THE BAR H miniseries, while award winner Ingrid Weaver checks in with *What the Baby Knew.* If it's edge-of-your-seat suspense you're looking for, pick up the latest from Sally Tyler Hayes, *Spies, Lies and Lovers.* *The Rancher's Surrender* is the latest from fresh new talent Jill Shalvis, while Shelley Cooper makes her second appearance with *Guardian Groom.*

You won't want to miss a single one of these fabulous novels, or any of the books we'll be bringing you in months to come. For guaranteed great reading, come to Silhouette Intimate Moments, where passion and excitement go hand in hand.

Enjoy!

Yours,

Leslie J. Wainger
Executive Senior Editor

Please address questions and book requests to:
Silhouette Reader Service
U.S.: 3010 Walden Ave., P.O. Box 1325, Buffalo, NY 14269
Canadian: P.O. Box 609, Fort Erie, Ont. L2A 5X3

A MAN OF HIS WORD

MERLINE LOVELACE

Published by Silhouette Books

America's Publisher of Contemporary Romance

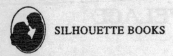

SILHOUETTE BOOKS

ISBN 0-373-07938-9

A MAN OF HIS WORD

Visit us at www.romance.net

Printed in U.S.A.

Books by Merline Lovelace

Silhouette Intimate Moments

Somewhere in Time #593
*Night of the Jaguar #637
*The Cowboy and the
   Cossack #657
*Undercover Man #669
*Perfect Double #692
†The 14th...and Forever #764
Return to Sender #866
**If a Man Answers #878
*The Mercenary and the
   New Mom* #908
**A Man of His Word #938

Silhouette Desire

Dreams and Schemes #872
†Halloween Honeymoon #1030
†Wrong Bride, Right Groom #1037
‡Undercover Groom #1220

Silhouette Books

Fortune's Children
Beauty and the Bodyguard

*Code Name: Danger
†Holiday Honeymoons
‡Fortune's Children: The Brides
**Men of the Bar H

MERLINE LOVELACE

After twenty-three years as an officer in the United States Air Force, Merline began an equally exciting second career as an author. When she's not glued to her keyboard, she and her own handsome hero, Al, enjoy traveling, golf and long, lively dinners with friends and family. They recently returned from a cruise to Alaska and are already planning a sail around the Mediterranean.

Merline enjoys hearing from readers and can be reached at P.O. Box 892717, Oklahoma City, OK 73189, or via Internet through Harlequin/Silhouette's web page at http://www.romance.net.

Prologue

Four of the five Henderson brothers stood in a loose semicircle, nursing chilled champagne while they watched their grinning brother waltz his bride of thirty minutes around the dance floor. Tall, tanned, each seasoned as much by his chosen profession as by his youth on the northern Arizona ranch they all still called home, they made a striking collection of broad shoulders, hard muscle and keen blue eyes.

Jake, the oldest of the five and the only other married Henderson male present, shook his head. "Still hard to believe it happened so fast. Of all of you, I expected Sam to hold out the longest. Instead he fell the hardest and the fastest. Molly's gonna lead that boy around more than the dance floor."

Tough, cynical Marsh, the middle brother, grunted in disgust. "He reminds me of your polled Herefords right now, Jake. Big, moon-faced and completely dehorned."

Even Evan had to agree. Smiling, the attorney tipped his glass in a salute to his newly married sibling. "Sam's got it bad, all right. He told me he would have strangled the bastard who came after Molly with his bare hands if the police hadn't arrived when they did."

Only Reece kept silent. Closest to Sam in both age and temperament, he wavered between a fierce happiness for his younger brother and an equally fierce hope that Sam and Molly could hang on to the love they didn't even try to disguise at this moment.

So few couples did.

Involuntarily his gaze shifted to the vibrant, laughing mother of the groom. Despite her dove-gray hair and the character lines that came with raising five boys and running a twenty-thousand-acre spread in the shadow of the rugged northern Arizona San Francisco Mountains, Jessica Henderson looked almost as young as Jake's wife, Ellen...and so unlike the woman who'd fallen apart one cold, February night that Reece's heart clenched.

None of his brothers knew about that night. About the terror of those dark, desperate hours, when Reece had come home unexpectedly between the engineering jobs that took him all over the world, and found his mother ravaged by loneliness and alcohol and a bitter, corrosive anger. She was almost incoherent when Reece arrived at the Bar-H, but she'd cried and clung to him, begged him not to call a doctor, not to shame her any more than she'd already been shamed.

A grim, shaken Reece had forced gallon after gallon of coffee down her throat. Walked her the length of the ranch house and back a thousand times. Listened to her wrenching sobs and searing anger at the husband she'd buried two years before.

That was when she told him about the letters she'd found hidden in a storage closet...and about the woman his father had carried on an affair with for years. At his mother's fierce insistence, Reece had burned the letters. Many of his illusions about marriage went up in smoke with those blue-edged notes.

Jessica Henderson had bottomed out that night, emptied the well of her self-pity and anger. Soon afterward, she'd turned the ranch over to Jake, who now managed it along with his own spread for the absent Henderson brothers. She'd bought a condo in Sedona and taken up golf, of all things. Now she traveled with her new friends and drove out to the ranch occasionally to visit the old ones. She'd put the terror of that cold, desperate February night behind her...as well as her anger at the husband who'd betrayed her.

Reece was still working on it.

Seeing his mother laughing and his younger brother grinning like a dope at his new bride helped.

What *didn't* help was knowing that Reece had to leave right after the reception to make the long drive back to the sleepy little town of Chalo Canyon in south-central Arizona because of an early-morning meeting with another determined home wrecker.

His champagne goblet hit the bar with a chink of crystal against wood. "I'm claiming a dance with my new sister-in-law," he told his brothers, "then I'm out of here."

Marsh lifted a brow. "You're not going to stay

and help us send Sam off on his honeymoon in the hallowed Henderson tradition?''

"Right," Jake drawled, "the 'hallowed' tradition you clowns started with me. Ellen still shudders when she remembers our wedding night."

"You boys will have to handle this one on your own," Reece said. "I have to be back on-site by dawn tomorrow. I've got a reservoir draining at the rate of eighty cubic feet per second and a dam with some cracks in it waiting for me."

Among other things.

His jaw tightened at the thought of the woman who'd pulled every string in the book to muscle her way into the restricted area behind the dam. She intended to shoot a documentary film of a sunken Anasazi village as it emerged from the waters of the reservoir, or so the letter from the Bureau of Reclamation directing Reece's cooperation had stated.

He knew better. She was returning to Chalo Canyon for one reason and one reason only...to finish what she'd started ten years ago. Everyone in town had told Reece so, including the man she'd begun the affair with.

Well, he didn't have to watch the woman in action. He'd meet with her bright and early tomorrow morning as promised. He'd advise her of his schedule, set some rules of engagement. Then she was on her own. He had more important matters to engage both his time and his attention than Sydney Scott.

Putting the woman firmly from his mind, Reece crossed the floor to claim a dance with his radiant new sister-in-law.

Chapter 1

Arms wrapped around her knees, Sydney sat bathed in warm summer moonlight on one of the limestone outcroppings that rimmed the Chalo River Reservoir. Although she couldn't see the movement, she knew the water level in the vast reservoir was slowly dropping. She'd been gauging its progress for hours now, measuring its descent against the shadowy crevasses on the cliff face opposite.

Another thirty-six hours, she estimated with a shiver of anticipation, forty-eight at most. Then the magical, mystical village she'd first seen as a child would emerge from the dark waters of the reservoir and feel the touch of the sun for the first time in a decade.

Once every ten years, the sluice gates of the dam that harnessed the Chalo River yawned fully open. Once every ten years, the man-made lake behind the dam was drained to allow maintenance and repair to the towering concrete structure. Once every ten years, the waters dropped and the ancient ruins reappeared. This was the year, the month, the week.

Excitement pulsed through Sydney's veins, excitement and a stinging regret that went soul deep.

"Oh, Dad," she murmured softly, "if only you'd had a few more months..."

No! No, she couldn't go down that road. She shook her head, fighting the aching sense of loss that had become so much a part of her she rarely acknowledged it anymore. She couldn't wish another day, another hour of that awful pain on her father. His death had been a release, a relief from the agony that even morphine couldn't dull. She wouldn't grieve for him now. Instead, she would use these quiet, moonlit hours to celebrate the times they'd been together.

With the perfect clarity of a camera lens, Sydney recalled her wide-eyed wonder when her father had first shown her the wet, glistening ruins tucked under a ledge in this small corner of Chalo Canyon. Then, as now, goose bumps had raised on her arms when the wind whispered through the canyon, sounding much like the Weeping Woman of local legend. According to the tale, an ancient Anasazi warrior had stolen a woman from another tribe and confined her in a stone tower in his village. The woman had cried for her lost love, and leaped to her death rather than submit to the man who'd taken her.

A youthful Sydney had heard the legend within days of moving to Chalo Canyon, where her father had taken over as fish and game warden for the state park that rimmed the huge, man-made lake behind the dam. Her dad had pooh-poohed the tale, but it had tugged at his daughter's imagination. So much so that she'd counted the years until she could capture the ruins on film as a special project for her cinematography class.

Sighing, Sydney rested her chin on her knees. How young she'd been then. How incredibly naive. A nineteen-year-old student at Southern Cal, she'd planned the film project all through her sophomore year. Couldn't wait for summer and the scheduled draining of the reservoir. Pop had gone with her that day, too, maneuvering the boat, keeping it steady while she balanced their home camcorder on her shoulder and shot the emerging village from every angle. Sydney had been so elated, so sure this project would be the start of a glorious career in film.

Then she'd tumbled head over heels in love with handsome, charming Jamie Chavez.

Even after all these years, the memory could still make Sydney writhe with embarrassment. Her breathless ardor had by turns amused and delighted the older, more sophisticated Jamie...much to his father's dismay. Sebastian Chavez's plans for his only son didn't include the daughter of the local fish and game warden.

Looking back, Sydney could only shake her head at her incredible stupidity. Jamie was more than willing to amuse himself with her while his fiancée was in Europe. Even now Sydney cringed when she remembered the night Sebastian found her in his son's bed. The scene had *not* been pretty. Even worse, the swing her father took at the powerful landowner the next day had cost him his job. The Scotts had moved away the following week, and neither of them had ever returned to Chalo Canyon.

Until now.

Now Sydney was about to see the ancient ruins for the third time. With a string of critically acclaimed documentaries and an Oscar nomination under her belt, she intended to capture the haunting ruins and the legend she'd first shared with her father so long ago on video- and audiotape. She'd worked for almost a year to script the project and secure funding. The final product would stand in loving tribute to the man who taught her the beauties and mysteries of Chalo Canyon.

Hopefully, she thought with a wry grimace, the documentary would also take her fledgling production company out of the red. Her father's long illness had cut both Sydney's heart and her financial resources to the quick. Even with the big-money financing her recent brush with the Oscars had generated, starting up her own production company had eaten what little was left of her savings. This project would make her or break her.

She brushed at a gnat buzzing her left ear, thinking of all the obstacles she'd overcome to get even this far. The preproduction work had taken almost eight months. She'd started on it just after her dad's leukemia robbed him of his breath and his mobility. She'd shared every step of the process with him during those long, agonizing hours at his bedside. Talked him through the concept. Described the treatment she envisioned, worked out an estimated budget. Then she'd hawked the idea to the History

Channel, to PBS, to half a dozen independent producers.

Pop's death had hardened Sydney's resolve into absolute determination to see the project through... despite Sebastian Chavez's vehement objections. When Sebastian heard of the proposed documentary, he'd used every weapon in his arsenal to kill it. He'd refused all access to the site through his land. He'd flexed his political muscle to delay filming permits. He'd even rallied Native American groups to protest the exploitation of sacred ruins. Evidently the hard feelings generated ten years ago hadn't died.

As a last-ditch attempt to block the project, Chavez had dragged the engineer in charge of the dam repair into the controversy and got him to weigh in against any activity in the restricted area behind the dam.

Sydney had played shamelessly on every connection she had from L.A. to D.C. to overturn Reece Henderson's nonconcurrence. Finally the powerful coalition of PBS, the National Historic Preservation Society, and her wealthy and well-known financial backer, who just happened to have contributed significantly to the president's reelection campaign, had prevailed.

As a condition of the approval, however, Sydney had to coordinate her filming schedule with the chief engineer and shoot around the blasting and repair work at the dam. Henderson's curt faxes in response to her initial queries had set her teeth on edge, but she refused to allow some bullheaded engineer to upset her or her tight schedule. She had only two weeks to capture a legend…and recapture the magic of her youth.

Her chin wobbled on her knees. Weariness tugged at the edges of her simmering anticipation. She should go back to the motel, grab a few hours of sleep before the rest of her crew arrived. She'd learned the hard way that rest and exercise were essential to countering the stress caused by tight schedules, the inevitable snafus, and the sheer physical and mental exhaustion of a shoot. Even more important, she'd need her wits and all her charm in full functioning order when she met with this Henderson guy in the morning.

She'd give herself just a few more moments, she decided. A last stretch of peace before the work began. A quiet time with her father and her dreams.

A rumble of thunder shattered the quiet less than a half hour later. All too soon the moon disappeared behind a pile of dark storm clouds

Sydney lifted her head, chewing on her lower lip as she eyed the lightning that lit the clouds from the inside out. Damned El Niño. Or maybe it was the depleted ozone layer that was causing the violent, unseasonable storms that had plagued the southwest this summer.

Whatever had spawned them, these storms could wreak havoc with her exterior shots, not to mention her shooting schedule. With luck, this one would break soon, dump its load, and move on so her crew could shoot their preparatory exterior tests tomorrow in bright sunshine. Sydney wanted light. She needed light. Light formed the essence of film and video imagery.

Scowling at another flash of white against the dark sky, she pushed to her feet and headed for her rented Chevy Blazer. She'd taken only a few steps when the wind picked up. The leaves on the cottonwoods lining the canyon rim rustled. The ends of the mink-brown hair tucked haphazardly under her L.A. Rams ball cap flicked against her cheek.

Suddenly, Sydney spun around, heart pounding. There it was! The sigh. The cry. The sob of the wind through the canyon.

Aiiiiii. Eee-aiiiii.

She stood frozen, letting the sound wrap around and through her. She could almost hear the despair behind the soughing sound, feel the unutterable sadness.

Another gust cut through the canyon, faster, deeper. The leaves whipped on the cottonwoods. The cry increased in pitch to a wail that lifted the fine hairs on the back of Sydney's neck.

Slowly, so slowly, the wind eased and the eerie lament faded.

"Now that," she muttered, rubbing the goose bumps that prickled every square inch of her bare arms, "was one heck of an audio bite. I wish to heck Albert had caught it."

Her soundman wouldn't arrive from L.A. until tomorrow noon, along with the camera operator and the grip she'd hired for this job. Only Sydney and her assistant, Zack, had come a day early—Sydney to snatch these few hours alone with her memories before the controlled chaos of the shoot began, Zack to finalize the motel and support arrangements he'd made by phone weeks ago.

Sydney could only hope the wind would perform for them again tomorrow afternoon when they shot the exterior setup sequences she'd planned—assuming, of course, this Reece Henderson approved her shooting schedule when she met with him in the morning.

Another frown creased her forehead as she dodged the first fat splats of rain on her way to her rented Blazer. She had enough documentaries under her belt to appreciate the intricacies of negotiating permits and approvals for an on-location shoot, but the requirement to coordinate her shooting schedule galled more than a little. Hopefully, this guy Henderson would prove more cooperative in person than he had by fax.

Sliding inside the Blazer, she shut out the now-pelting rain and groped for the keys in the pockets of the military fatigue pants she bought by the dozen at an Army-Navy surplus store in south L.A. The baggy camouflage pants didn't exactly shout Rodeo Drive chic, but Sydney had found their tough construction and many pockets a godsend on isolated shoots like this one.

One foot on the clutch, the other on the brake, she keyed the ignition and wrapped a hand around the shift knob, wishing fervently she'd thought to specify automatic drive before Zack arranged for rental vehicles. From the way the gears ground when she tried to coax them into first, the Blazer obviously wished so, too.

"Sorry," she muttered, working the clutch and the stick again.

After another protesting *snnnrck,* the gears engaged. With rain pinging steadily against the roof, Sydney eased the Blazer onto the road. She kept her foot light on the accelerator and her eyes on the treacherous curves ahead.

Little more than a dirt track, Canyon Rim Road snaked along the canyon's edge for miles before joining the state road that accessed the dam. The stone outcroppings that edged the road on the left made every turn a real adventure. The sheer drop on the right added to the pucker factor. The deluge that poured out of the black sky didn't exactly help either visibility or navigability. Chewing on her lower lip, Sydney downshifted and took a hairpin turn at a crawl.

A few, tortuous turns later she was forced to admit that it might have made more sense to wait until daylight to drive along the canyon rim. She'd needed this time alone with her memories, though. And there'd been no indication earlier that a storm might—

"What the—!"

She came out of a sharp turn and stomped on the brake. Or what she thought was the brake. Her boot hit the clutch instead, and the Blazer rolled straight at the slab of rock that had tumbled onto the road from the outcropping beside it.

Choking back an oath, Sydney swung both her foot and the wheel. With the rock wall on the left and the sheer drop-off on the right, there was no room to maneuver around the obstacle. The Blazer

swung too far out before she jammed on the brake
and stopped its roll.

To her horror, she felt the road's narrow shoulder
begin to crumble under the Blazer's weight. The vehicle lurched back, dropped at an angle, stalled. Frantic, Sydney dragged the stick back to neutral, twisted
the key.

"Come on! Come on!"

The engine turned over at the exact moment another piece of the rim gave. The four-wheel tilted at
a crazy angle and started to slide backward.

"Oh, God!"

Shouldering open the door, Sydney threw herself
out. She hit on one hip and twisted desperately,
scrabbling for purchase on the rain-slick earth. Beside her the Blazer gave a fearsome imitation of the
Titanic. Metal groaned against sandstone. Nose up,
headlights stabbing the rain, it slid backward like the
great ship slipping into its dark grave, then slowly
toppled over the edge.

The echoes of its crashing descent were still ringing in Sydney's ears when sandstone and muddy
earth crumbled under her frantic fingers and she followed the Blazer over the edge.

Reece Henderson slapped a rolled-up schematic of
the Chalo River Dam against his jeans-clad thigh.
Jaw tight, he waited while the phone he held to his
ear shrilled a half dozen times. He'd started to slam
it down when the receiver was fumbled off the hook.
Reece took the mumbled sound on the other end for
a hello.

"Where is she?"

"Huh?"

"Where's Scott?"

"Whoziz?"

Gripping the receiver in a tight fist, Reece glared at the mirrored calendar on the opposite wall of the office set aside for his use.

"This is Henderson, Reece Henderson. Chief engineer on the Chalo River Dam project. Where's your boss?"

"Dunno." There was a jaw-cracking yawn at the other end of the line. "What time izit?"

"Eight forty-seven," he snapped. "She was supposed to be here at eight."

The irritation that had started simmering at 8:05 was now at full boil. He'd hung around topside waiting for the blasted woman, wasting almost an hour he could have spent down inside the dam with his engineers.

"Did you, like, try her room?" The kid at the other end of the line sounded more alert now, if not more coherent.

"Yes. Twice. There wasn't any answer. The motel operator said you were her assistant and would know where she was."

Actually, Martha Jenkins, who pulled triple duty as owner, operator and day clerk at the Lone Eagle Motel, had provided Reece with more details than he'd either asked for or wanted. Martha hadn't been on duty when Sydney Scott and her gum-popping, green-haired, multiple-body-pierced assistant Zachary Tyree checked in late yesterday afternoon, but things got around fast in a town the size of Chalo Canyon.

"Hang loose."

The phone clattered down. The sound of sheets whooshing aside was followed in quick succession by the snick of a zipper and padding footsteps. Long moments later the phone rattled again.

"She's not in her room."

Reece rolled his eyes. He thought they'd already established that fact.

"Well, if she strolls in anytime soon, tell her I left my brother's wedding early and drove half the night so I would make the meeting she didn't bother to show for. She can call me here at the site. I'll get back to her when and if…"

"You don't understand, dude. She's not here."

Reece felt the last of his patience shredding. "Tell your boss—"

"The blinds in her room were open and I looked in. Her bed hasn't been slept in."

Worry put a crack in the kid's voice. A different sort of emotion put a lock on Reece's jaw.

God! He'd been hearing the rumors and gossip about this Scott woman for weeks. How she'd thrown herself at Jamie Chavez ten years ago. How Jamie's father had all but dragged her out of his son's bed. How *her* father had knocked Chavez, Sr., on his butt the next day. Now she was a big, important Hollywood director, coming back to Chalo River to impress everyone with her success…and to try her luck with Jamie again.

Reece couldn't suppress the disgust that swirled in his gut. The woman had arrived in town only yesterday afternoon and had already spent the night somewhere other than her motel room. Pretty fast work, even for a big, important Hollywood director.

Well, Reece had complied with his boss's direct communiqué. He'd cooperated with the woman, or tried to, damn near busting his butt to get back here in time for their meeting this morning. The ball was in Ms. Sydney Scott's court now, and she could lob it at the net from now until next Christmas for all he cared. He started to hang up when the sharp concern in the kid's voice stilled his hand.

"Syd drove out to the canyon right after we got settled here at the motel yesterday afternoon. She could still be out there."

"What?"

Reece's irritation spiked into anger. He'd made it plain to Ms. Scott in their exchange of faxes that neither she nor any of her crew should go poking around in the restricted area behind the dam until he briefed them on the repair project and the potential hazards during the blasting period.

"Syd said she wanted to check the water level in the reservoir and get her bearings. Told me not to wait up for her. You don't think she, like, got lost or something?"

"I understand Ms. Scott used to live in this area. She should know her way around."

"That was ten years ago, dude."

"The name's Henderson."

"Right, Henderson. Could you, like, drive around and check on her? She sorta gets involved in her projects sometimes and forgets what day it is. I'd go myself, but I don't know the geography, and Syd's got the Blazer, which leaves me, like, without wheels until Tish and the others get here.''

Reece wanted very much to tell the kid what he and his boss could, like, do, but he'd assumed responsibility for this project and all the challenges and headaches that went with it. Including, it appeared, Sydney Scott. If she'd entered the restricted area and gotten her vehicle stuck in the mud after that gully-washer last night, she was, unfortunately, his problem.

''All right. I'll drive along the rim and look for her. Take down my mobile phone number. If she walks in, call me.''

''Thanks, man!''

After a call down to his second-in-charge to advise him that he'd be on mobile for the next half hour or so, Reece exchanged his hard hat for a battered straw Stetson, legacy of those rare breaks between jobs which he spent at the Bar-H, helping his brother Jake. A moment later, he left the air-conditioned comfort of the office for the blazing heat of a summer Arizona sun bouncing off concrete.

The administration building perched on the east end of the dam, a massive concrete arch that thrust its arms against the steep Chalo Canyon walls. Some 305 feet below, two fully opened spillways poured tons of rushing water into the lower Chalo. Tipping his hat forward to shade his eyes, Reece paused for a moment to assess the reservoir behind the dam. All traces of the thunderstorm that had lashed the area last night had disappeared. Sunlight sparkled on the water's surface, already, he noted with grim satisfaction, sunk well below its usual level.

By tomorrow, he should be able to examine from the outside the cracks that had started stressing the dam from the inside. He'd know then how much work he had ahead of him, and how long this Sydney Scott would have to film her documentary before the reservoir started filling again.

Assuming, of course, that she'd intended to make a movie at all. Maybe the rumors were true. Maybe this documentary was just a smoke screen, a convenient cover for her personal intentions. Maybe she'd really come back to Chalo River to make nothing but trouble.

If that was the case, she was off to a helluva good start. When and if Reece located Ms. Scott, she might just realize she'd bitten off more trouble than she could chew this time.

He found her twenty minutes later. Or more correctly, he found the spot where the canyon rim had crumbled, taking half the road with it.

Chapter 2

"Hey! You down there! Are you okay?"

The shout jerked Sydney's head back. Never in her life had she heard anything as wonderful as that deep, gruff voice. Keeping a tight grip on the twisted piñon tree that had broken her slide into oblivion seven long hours ago, she shouted to the dark-haired cowboy peering cautiously over the edge of the rim.

"I'm okay. No broken bones that I can tell. Have you got a rope?"

"Yes. I'll be right back. Don't move!"

Don't move. Right. As if she planned on releasing her death grip on the rough-barked trunk or shifting her body so much as a centimeter to either side of the narrow toehold she'd found in the canyon wall.

She leaned her forehead against the tree, almost giddy with relief. Then again, this dizzy sensation might have something to do with the fact that she'd just spent seven hours wedged between a tree root and a cliff face hundreds of feet above a narrow river gorge.

She'd been prepared to spend even longer. Sydney hadn't expected Zack to roll out of bed before ten or eleven, much less organize a rescue for his missing boss. Her assistant was worth his 140 pounds in gold once he revved his motor, but getting him going some mornings could take a half-dozen calls that ran the gamut from wheedling to cajoling to outright threats of death and dismemberment. Thank God this was one of his rare self-starting days!

The thump of a rope hitting against the cliff face above her snapped her attention back to the rim. She looked up just in time to take the shower of small stones and dust dislodged by the rope full in her face. Wincing, Sydney spun her head sideways, which caused the tree to shake and its occupant to let out a small, terrified squeak.

"Dammit, don't move!" her rescuer snapped. "I'll work the rope over to you."

Clinging to the tree trunk with both arms, she blew upward in a vain attempt to get the dust and straggling hair out of her eyes. Her Rams ball cap had gone the way of the Blazer during that three-second slide down the cliff face. Sydney only hoped the sacrifice of a hat and a four-wheel-drive vehicle had satisfied the canyon gods.

Her heart in her throat, she watched the thick rope hump and bump its way closer to her precarious perch. Only after it was within reach did she discover that her arms were numb from the shoulders down.

She couldn't seem to unlock their tight grip on the trunk.

"Take the rope."

Swiping her tongue along dry lips, she tried again. Her left arm came unwrapped and dangled like overcooked linguini at her side.

"I need a minute here," she croaked to her rescuer. "I can't seem to feel my arms."

"All right, it's all right." The gruff voice above her gentled. "Don't worry about it."

"Easy for you to say," Sydney muttered to the piñon, her eyes on the rope a tantalizing few inches away. Suddenly it jounced up and out of sight.

"Hey!"

"Hang on, I'm coming down."

He pulled off his hat and looped the rope around his waist. Within moments he was beside her. Black hair ruffled. Blue eyes steady and encouraging in a tanned face. Shoulders roped with reassuringly thick cords of muscle. Altogether he looked big, strong and wonderfully solid.

On second thought, Sydney wasn't so sure big and solid were desirable characteristics in a man whose only connection to terra firma was a length of twisted hemp. Swallowing, she said a silent prayer for the sureness of his lifeline while he propped his boots against the canyon wall. With a cowboy's one-handed ease, he shook out a loop in the length of rope he'd left dangling behind him.

"Bend your head. Let me slip this over you." He spoke slowly, his deep voice calm, confident. "I'm going to lift one of your arms. Got a grip? Okay, now the other. Easy, easy."

The noose tightened around her waist, cutting off most of her breath. The taut, muscled arm the stranger slid around her cut off the rest.

"I've got you. I'm going to swing you in front of me. We'll walk up the cliff face together. Ready?"

Even with the rope and her rescuer's muscled arm around her, it took a considerable leap of faith to let go of the sturdy little piñon. Swallowing hard, she let him lift her from the tree.

"I've got you. I won't let go."

She managed a shaky laugh. "Promise?"

"I'm a man of my word," he assured her, his breath warm in her ear.

She hoped so. She certainly hoped so.

"Ready?"

She gulped. "Ready."

They crab-walked up the cliff, her bottom nested against his stomach, his arms caging her ribs. Five steps, seven, eight, then a palm on her rear and a heaving shove.

Sydney went over the rim belly down. Panting, she crawled on hands and knees until the ground felt firm enough for her to turn and try to help her rescuer over the edge. Her arms were still so weak she gave up after the first useless tug.

Not that he appeared to need any assistance. With a smooth coordination of brawn and grace, he hauled himself up. Once safely away from the crumbled rim, he untied his lifeline and strode to the Jeep that had anchored it. Sydney gave a little croak of delight when he hunkered down beside her a moment later, a plastic bottle of spring water in his hand. She downed a half dozen greedy gulps before coming up for air. After another swallow or two, her throat had loosened enough to talk without croaking.

"Thanks…for the water and the rescue."

"You're welcome." He picked up his hat and dusted it against his thigh before settling it on his head. "Sure you're not hurt?"

"Just a little weak from hanging on to the tree all night. I collected a few dents and scrapes on my way down, but nothing that won't heal or cover up."

His blue eyes raked her over from the top of her dusty head to the toes of her dusty boots, performing their own assessment. Evidently he agreed with her diagnosis.

"I saw the wreckage at the bottom of the gorge. What happened?"

"There was a boulder in the road. With the rain, I didn't see in time and swung too sharply. I got out of the Blazer before it went over, but the rim crumbled beneath me. I thought… I was sure…" She substituted a wobbly smile for the shudder she wanted to let rip. "The piñon broke my fall. How does that poem go, the one about never seeing anything as beautiful as a tree?"

"Beats me." He studied her from under the brim of that beat-up hat, his expression noticeably less comforting and reassuring now that they were back on solid ground. "You're a lucky woman."

She started to point out that not everyone would classify someone who went over a cliff as lucky, but his next comment buried the thought.

"And damned stupid."

"I beg your pardon?"

"Most people would have more sense than to

drive along a narrow canyon rim road late at night in the middle of a thunderstorm.''

Sydney had come to the same conclusion herself just before she went bungee jumping without a bungee, but she didn't particularly enjoy hearing it from someone else. Still, he'd plucked her out of her eagle's nest. She owed him, big-time.

Ordering her arms and legs to do their thing, she pushed herself to her feet. Her rescuer had to shoot out a hand and catch her before she whumped back down on her rear. Shaking off his hand, she tried to sound grateful.

''Thanks. Again. I'm Sydney Scott, by the way.''

''I know who you are.''

She flushed at the drawled response, feeling even more stupid than he'd implied earlier. If he was part of a search party, of course he'd know who he'd come looking for.

''And you are?''

''Reece Henderson.''

''Oh.'' The straw Stetson that shaped his head as if made for it had led her to assume he was a local. ''You're the dam engineer.''

From the way his eyes narrowed, she must have put a little too much emphasis on *dam*. Either that, or their exchange of terse faxes had annoyed him as much as it had her.

''When you didn't show for our meeting this morning,'' he said curtly, ''I called your assistant and woke him up.''

So much for the massive search-and-rescue effort Sydney had assumed Zack set in motion!

''The kid told me you'd driven out to the canyon.

He seemed to think you might have fallen into an artistic trance and gotten lost."

"I don't fall into artistic trances," she said with another smile, slightly strained but still trying hard for grateful.

One black brow lifted in patent disbelief.

"All right," she admitted grudgingly, "I did leave a pot of red beans and rice on the stove a couple of months ago while I was working a treatment, but the fire didn't do any real damage."

When he only looked at her through those cool blue eyes, Sydney gave Zack a mental kick in the shins. How much had her assistant told this guy, anyway?

"Maybe I did start out for San Diego last week and didn't realize I was going in the wrong direction until I passed Santa Barbara," she said defensively, "but I was outlining a script in my mind and sort of got caught up in it."

With a little snort that sounded suspiciously like disgust, her rescuer strolled back to the Jeep to untie the rope. "Is that what you were doing last night when you drove off a cliff?"

"I was *not* in any kind of a trance last night."

Well, she amended silently, maybe she had let her imagination go for a while, particularly when the wind whistled eerily through the canyon and raised goose bumps all over her body. Henderson didn't need to know that, though.

"As I told you, there was a boulder in the road, a chunk of sandstone. I swerved to avoid it."

"If you say so, lady."

Gratitude was getting harder and harder to hang

on to. Sydney folded her arms across her now-scruffy yellow T-shirt.

"I do say so."

He straightened, the rope half-looped in his hand, his eyes as sharp and slicing as lasers. "Then maybe you'll also tell me why you were driving around in a restricted area without a permit? A permit that I had intended to issue at our meeting this morning, by the way."

That "had intended" caught Sydney's attention and shoved everything else out of her mind. The terror of sliding over a cliff, the long, frightening hours alone with only a piñon tree for company, the crab-walk up a sheer rock wall fell away. All that remained was her absolute determination to capture the magic of the ruins on videotape...for her dad, for herself, for the joys and tears they'd shared.

Every inch a professional now, she cut right to the heart of the issue. "I apologize for going around you, Mr. Henderson. I arrived in Chalo Canyon earlier than planned yesterday afternoon. I tried to contact you for permission to drive out to the site, but you were out of town. At a wedding, or so they told me."

"So you drove out, anyway."

"*After* I talked to one of your engineers. He said he thought it would be okay. I believe his name was Patrick Something."

It would be Patrick, Reece thought in disgust. Young, breezy, overconfident of his brand-new civil engineering degree that hadn't yet been tested by thousands of tons of wet concrete and millions of yards of rushing water. Reece finished looping the rope.

"Apology accepted this time, Ms. Scott. Just don't go around me again. I'm chief engineer on this project. The responsibility for the safety of everyone involved, including you and your crew, rests with me."

"It's Sydney," she returned, seething inside at the undeserved lecture, but determined to hammer out a working relationship with this bullheaded engineer.

"Sydney," he acknowledged with a little nod. "Now we'd better get you back to town so you can have those scrapes and dents checked out. In the meantime, I'll get hold of the county sheriff and let him know about the accident."

"I'd prefer to conduct our planned discussion before I hitch a ride into town. If this sunlight holds and the rest of my crew arrives on time, I want to shoot some exterior footage this afternoon."

Reece stared at her across the Jeep's hood. For God's sake, was she for real? She'd just spent the night perched in a tree. Her baggy fatigue pants and yellow T-shirt looked like they'd been worn by someone on the losing side of the last war. Her tangled, dark brown mane hung in rats' tails on either side of her face...a face, he admitted reluctantly, made remarkable by wide green eyes, high cheekbones and a mouth a man could weave some pretty lurid fantasies around.

Not Reece. Not after all he'd heard about Sydney Scott. He'd make damned sure he didn't weave fantasies of any kind about this particular package of trouble. That tug he felt low in his belly was grudging admiration for her sheer guts, nothing more.

"All right. We'll drive back to the dam and go over schedules." He reached into the Jeep and tossed her the mobile phone. "Here, you'd better call your assistant and let him know you're okay while I block the road."

With the rope looped over one arm, he rooted around in the back of the Jeep for the toolbox he never traveled without. Inside was a thick roll of electrical tape. It wasn't red, but it would have to do as a hazard warning until he could get a crew out here to erect permanent barriers.

"Zack? It's Sydney."

Her voice carried to him at the rear of the Jeep, attractive enough now that most of the croak had disappeared.

"No, I didn't get lost. I, er, drove off a cliff."

She caught Reece's sardonic look and turned her back.

"Yes, I'm fine. Really. Honest. I swear. Just get hold of the insurance company, okay? Make sure our on-location liability coverage extends to rented Blazers that now reside at the bottom of a river gorge. And arrange for another vehicle. I want to do some site shots this afternoon."

Reece turned away, shaking his head. This was one single-minded female. He'd remember that in future dealings with her.

"It's a long story," she told her assistant, scooping her tangled hair back with one hand. "I'll fill you in on the details later. What have you heard from Tish and the others? Noon? Good! Tell them to be ready to roll as soon as I get back. What time is it now?"

Her little screech of dismay followed Reece to the vertical outcropping a few yards away. Reddish lime-

stone striated with yellow and green pushed upward.
Hardened by nature, sculpted by time, it formed a
wall of oddly shaped rock. Too often wind and rain
toppled smaller segments of these formations and
sent them tumbling down, which in turn caused bigger pieces to break off.

Pale gashes showed where the rock had broken
loose last night. Reece fingered the marks, frowning,
then surveyed what remained of the road at this
point. The stone formations butted out, making it almost impossible to see around the curve. A driver
couldn't have chosen a worse point to go head-to-
head with a fallen rock.

Edging past the narrow neck, he blocked the road
off from the other side. He did the same on the Jeep
side. His insides still were tight from the narrowness
of her escape when he returned.

Sydney buried a sigh at the scowl on her rescuer's
face as he strode toward her. She had to work with
this guy for the next few weeks. They were not, she
decided, going to rank up there among the most en-
joyable weeks of her life. With any luck, she and
Henderson wouldn't have to see each other again after today.

That hope sustained her during the short, silent
ride to the Chalo River Dam. She'd seen the massive
structure many times before, of course. During the
years her father had served as fish and game warden
for the state park that enclosed the reservoir, he'd
taken her by boat and by car when he went to check
water levels and shoot the breeze with the power
plant operators.

And when the reservoir had been emptied ten years ago, leaving the dam naked and glistening in the sun, she'd attempted to capture its utilitarian starkness as well as the Anasazi ruins on film. Of course, she remembered with a wry twist of her lips, that was before her foolish infatuation with Jamie Chavez had blurred both her vision and her purpose.

She didn't have that problem now. Now she saw the curved structure through an artist's eye trained to recognize beauty in its most elemental state. The contrast of whitened concrete against reddish-yellow cliffs made her hands itch for a camera. The symmetry of the arch, with its gated spillways flanking each abutment, pleased her sense of proportion.

The air-conditioned chill of the administration building pleased her even more. Sydney took a moment for her eyes to adjust from dazzling sunlight to dim interior before accepting the mug Reece handed her.

"Thanks."

"You'd better save your thanks until you taste what's in it," he commented dryly. "My guys swear they can use this stuff to patch the dam if we run short of concrete."

The sludgelike coffee carried enough caffeine to make it worth the effort of swallowing.

"Speaking of patching," Sydney hinted broadly, "when do you plan to start?"

He shot her another of those sardonic looks, and gestured to a government-issue metal chair beside an equally nondescript desk. She carried her coffee over with her, careful to keep it away from the charts and clipboards precisely aligned on the desktop.

Tossing his hat aside, Henderson forked his fingers through his pelt of black hair before pulling out one of the clipboards. The tanned skin at the corners of his eyes crinkled with concentration as he skimmed an acetate status sheet filled with grease-pencil markings.

"The water passed the halfway mark just after 6:00 a.m. this morning."

Sydney attempted a quick a mental calculation. The village nestled in an opening in the cliff face fifty feet or so above the riverbed. If the waters had receded halfway down the cliff face already, they'd reach the ruins when? Eight tomorrow morning? Nine?

Hell! There was a reason she'd routinely cut her science and math classes in college and now carried a really good calculator in her purse at all times. The problem was that at this particular moment both purse and calculator rested amid the wreckage of the Blazer.

"When can I expect to see the ruins?"

"If we don't get any more storms like last night's, the reservoir should empty down to the river level by noon tomorrow. The cave that contains the ruins is some fifty feet above the riverbed. I calculate the village will start to emerge at approximately 9:24."

"Nine twenty-four? Not 9:23, huh? I could probably use that extra minute."

He didn't appear to appreciate her feeble attempt at humor. "I'm an engineer. Precision ranks right up there with timeliness in our book. And safety." He leveled her a sardonic look. "Try not to drive off any more cliffs, Ms. Scott."

"Sydney," she reminded him, shrugging off the sarcasm as her mind whirled. Thinking of the exterior scenes she wanted to shoot this afternoon and the sequencing for tomorrow's all-important emergence, she only half absorbed Reece's deep voice.

"We've detected a stress fracture on the right lower quadrant of the dam's interior. Depending on my exterior damage assessment, we may have to blast some of the old section and pour new concrete. Check in with me each morning before you come out to the site, and I'll let you know the status and whether I want you in the restricted area."

That got her attention.

"Each morning?" she yelped. "What happened to your engineering precision here? I need a little more notice than that to plan my daily takes."

"Call me the night before, then. That's the best I can do until we complete the damage assessment."

"Okay, okay. Give me your number. My little black book with all my contacts is at the bottom of the gorge right now."

Along with all her working files. Thank goodness she always kept complete electronic records of her projects on her laptop, which she'd left back at the motel. She patted her pockets, searching for a pencil before borrowing one from the holder on the desk. Like all the others in the round holder, it was sharpened to a razor tip—another engineering quirk, she guessed.

"You can reach me at the office, on my mobile, or at the Lone Eagle Motel."

Sydney scribbled down the numbers as he reeled them off. "That's where we're staying, too."

"I know."

The dry response brought her head up.

"Chalo Canyon's a small town, Ms. Scott... Sydney. That's the only motel in town."

She was well aware of that fact. She was also aware, as well, of the slight chill in his voice. She had a good idea what had caused it.

"And?" she asked coolly.

His broad shoulders lifted in a shrug. "And people in small towns like to talk, even to strangers. I've been hearing about your return to the Chalo Canyon for several weeks now."

"About my departure from said canyon ten years ago, you mean?"

He leaned back, his long legs sprawled under the desk. The chair squeaked with his weight as he regarded her through eyes framed by ridiculously thick black lashes.

"That, too."

Sydney had come a long way from the hopelessly romantic nineteen-year-old. She wasn't running away this time, from Sebastian or Jamie or herself. Nor, she decided grimly, from this chief engineer.

"Listen, Mr. Henderson..."

"Reece."

"Listen, Reece. What happened ten years ago is, if you'll excuse the lame pun, water over the dam. Something I'd like very much to forget."

"Folks around here seem to want to remember it."

"That's their problem, not mine." She leaned forward, jabbing the air with the pencil to emphasize her point. "And even though it's none of your business, I'll tell you that the only reason I came back to Chalo Canyon is to capture the ruins on videotape. I started the project a decade ago. This time I intend to finish it.''

He studied her through hooded eyes. "Why is this particular project so important to you that you'd spend ten years planning it?''

Sydney forced down the lump that tried to climb into her throat. Her father's death was too recent, the scar still too raw, to talk about it with strangers.

"I'm a documentarian," she said with a tight edge to her voice. "Like you, I take great pride in my work. By themselves, the ruins emerging from their long sleep make a good story. Supplemented with historical background material on the Anasazi and the legend of the Weeping Woman of Chalo Canyon, I can craft a good story into a great one.''

She pushed to her feet.

"Now if you don't mind, I'd like to hitch a ride back to town. The rest of my crew is supposed to arrive around noon, and I want to be ready to roll as soon as they get here.''

It was, Reece decided as he watched her drive off with one of his underlings, an impressive performance.

He might even have believed her if he hadn't been sitting front row, center stage when she made her grand entrance at the Lone Eagle Café some eight hours later.

Chapter 3

Like the clientele it catered to, the Lone Eagle Café made no pretensions to elegance. Most of its business came from locals, the rest from pleasure boaters and fishermen who passed through town on their way to or from excursions on the vast man-made lake behind the dam. Occasionally work crews hunkered in and made the motel and café their headquarters during visits to the hydroelectric plant powered by the Chalo River.

Reece had stayed at the motel during his initial site survey last winter and again during the pre-planning phase of the dam's inspection and repair a few months ago. He'd returned three weeks ago to supervise the project itself. By now he pretty well knew the café's menu by heart, and had settled on the rib-eye steak and pinto beans as his standard fare.

The beef came from Sebastian Chavez's spread

north of town, or so he'd been told by the friendly, broad-hipped Lula Jenkins, who, along with her sister, Martha, co-owned and operated the Lone Eagle Motel and Café. The pinto beans, Lula had advised, were grown on a local farm irrigated by water from the Chalo River Reservoir.

"And if you want to keep on shoveling in these beans," she reminded Reece as she plunked his overflowing plate down in front of him, "you'd better see that you get that reservoir filled in time for the fall planting."

"Yes, ma'am."

"Folks hereabouts depend on that water. Depend on the revenues from boaters and fishermen, too."

"I know."

Inviting herself to join him, Lula eased her comfortable bulk into the chair opposite Reece's. Her heavy-lidded brown eyes, evidence of the Native American heritage shared by so many in this region, drilled him from across the green-and-white-checkered plastic tablecloth.

"How long will it take to restock the reservoir with fish after you boys get done messing with the dam?"

Reece's nostrils twitched at the tantalizing aroma rising from his steak. He hadn't eaten since his hurried breakfast of diced-ham-and-egg burritos, wolfed down during the drive out to the dam just after dawn this morning. Despite the rumbling in his stomach, however, he knew his dinner would have to wait a while longer. Lula's question wasn't an idle one. It echoed the worries of a small town that depended on the Chalo River Reservoir for its livelihood.

Reece had prepared detailed environmental-and economic-impact assessments as part of his prep work for the repair project. He'd also conducted a series of meetings with local business and property owners to walk concerned parties through the process, step by step. Slides and briefings didn't carry quite the same impact for the people involved as seeing their water supply disappear before their eyes, though.

As the nation's fifth-largest electric utility and the second-largest wholesale water supplier, the Bureau of Reclamation's network of dams and reservoirs generated more than forty billion kilowatt-hours of electricity and delivered over ten trillion gallons of water each year. One out of five farmers in the western states depended on this water for irrigation to produce their crops. Additionally, hundreds of thousands of sports fishermen and recreationists plied the man-made lakes behind the dams, contributing their share to the economic fabric of communities like Chalo Canyon.

Even more important, the dams harnessed rivers like the Salt and the Gila and the mighty Colorado, controlling the floods and the devastation they'd wrought over the centuries. Born and bred to the West, Reece had grown up with a healthy respect for a river's power. In college he'd double-majored in civil and hydroelectric engineering. After college he'd worked dam projects all over the world. His father's death and the itch to get back to the vast, rugged West where he'd grown to manhood had led to a position with the Bureau of Reclamation's Structural Analysis Group in Denver. The Chalo River inspection and repair project had brought him home to Arizona.

Patiently he addressed Lula's concerns about the project's impact on the serious business of pleasure boating and sports fishing. "My headquarters in Washington began coordinating this project more than a year ago with the U.S. Fish and Wildlife Service and the Arizona Fish and Game Department. The government facility at Willow Bend has doubled its rainbow trout output to resupply the reservoir. The state hatchery will restock channel catfish, black crappie, perch and striped bass. The take won't be as plentiful for a year or more after the lake refills, but it should still provide enough catch to bring in the sport fishermen."

"It better," Lula grumbled. "Things are lookin' pretty thin now, I can tell you. Martha said she doesn't have a single room reserved after your crew and Miss Fancy-Pants Scott's folks leave." The waitress shook her head. "Imagine her driving right off a cliff!"

Reece took a long pull on his beer while Lula rambled on about the accident. Fancy-Pants wasn't exactly how he'd categorize the woman he'd pulled out of a piñon tree this morning. Unless, of course, she wore something decidedly provocative under those baggy U.S. Army rejects.

An image of the leggy, tousle-haired brunette in lacy black bikini briefs flashed into his mind for an instant. Resolutely Reece pushed it out. What she wore or didn't wear under her fatigues was none of his business. His only concern was the safety of her and her crew during their filming around the dam site.

The same couldn't be said for everyone else in town. The imminent arrival of the filmmaker and her crew had dominated the conversation at the café and the town's only bar for weeks. Everyone had an opinion about why she'd come back, and most were only too willing to voice it. Clearly ready for another discourse on the prodigal's return, Lula flapped a hand at Reece.

"Go on, go on, eat that steak while it's still sizzlin'. I'm just keepin' you company while I'm waitin' for them Hollywood people. Did you know that boy with the Scott woman has rings through every part of him that moves, and a few that don't?"

Reece sawed into his steak, not particularly interested in a discussion of Zack Tyree's body parts. It took more than a disinterested grunt, however, to discourage the garrulous Lula.

"Martha says she sneaked a peek at him when she went in to change the bed linens this morning. Couldn't hardly miss him, really. He was prowling around buck naked, wearin' nothing but them rings."

Thankfully, the sound of the door opening sent his hostess swiveling around. A grin beamed across her broad face.

"Hey, Jamie! You're lookin' good, boy, as always."

Tanned, golden-haired Jamie Chavez ushered his wife into the café and guided her across the room to Reece's table.

"Hey, Lula. You're lookin' beautiful, as always."

His smile shifted to include her customer. "How's the spill going, Henderson?"

Reece got to his feet, taking the hand Chavez offered in a firm grip.

"It's going," he replied easily. "Another hundred and fifty feet to river level. Nice to see you again, Mrs. Chavez."

The rail-thin redhead at Jamie's side smiled. "Please, call me Arlene. After all the hours you've spent out at the ranch, briefing Jamie and my father-in-law on the dam project, I think we can dispense with formalities."

She was even thinner than Reece remembered from his last visit. Her feathery auburn hair framed sunken cheekbones and hollowed eyes. Skillful makeup softened the stark angles of her face, and her natural elegance drew attention away from her gauntness, but Reece glimpsed the same desperate unhappiness in her shadowed eyes as he'd seen in his mother's not long ago.

Both women had learned to live with the fact that the man they loved had cheated on them. His mother found out about her husband's infidelity after his death. Jamie's transgression occurred during his engagement to Arlene, if the tales of ten years ago held any truth. Now that long-buried embarrassment had come back to haunt her.

Reece had to admit the green-eyed brunette he'd walked up a canyon wall this morning could certainly give this woman something to worry about. Sympathy for the worried wife tugged at him as Lula heaved herself to her feet.

"Did you two come in for dinner? I've got some

prime rib-eye in the cooler that was wearin' the Chavez brand not too long ago. I laid in an extra supply for those Hollywood folks, but they said they'd eat light when they got back tonight, whatever 'light' means," she grumbled.

"Probably tofu and soybean salad," Jamie teased.

"Ha!" Lula hitched her apron on her ample hips. "If they're expectin' tofu and such, they're sure as hell not gonna find it at the Lone Eagle Café."

"Where are they?" Jamie asked casually.

Too casually, Reece thought. Arlene evidently thought so, too. She threw her husband a sharp glance.

"Well, they loaded up two vans and took off just after one," Lula told him. "Said they'd be back after the light went, though, so I expect them anytime. If they aren't gonna eat those steaks, I gotta do something with them. What do you say I throw two on the grill for you and the missus?"

Arlene shook her head. "No, thanks. We just stopped by to—"

"Sure," her husband interrupted genially. "Why not? Bring out two more of those beers, too."

"But, Jamie…"

"We don't have to get back to the ranch right away, darling. Mind if we join you, Henderson?"

Reece shrugged. "Of course not. Please, be my guest."

A tight-lipped Arlene slid into the chair he held out for her. She didn't want a steak. That much was obvious. From the nervous glances she darted at the front door every time it opened, it was also obvious she didn't want to be sitting at the Lone Eagle Café when the Hollywood folks, as Lula termed them, returned.

Reece reminded himself that neither Jamie Chavez, his wife, nor the woman who'd almost come between them were any of his business, but that didn't kill the little stab of pity he felt for Arlene when the door swung open twenty minutes later and Sydney trooped in with her crew.

They were certainly a colorful bunch, from the kid with the green hair and the be-ringed nostrils to the statuesque, ebony-skinned six-footer who toted camera bags over each shoulder and sported a turquoise T-shirt with Through a Lens Lightly emblazoned in glittering gold across her magnificent chest. The guy with the earphones draped around his neck like stethoscopes was obviously the soundman. The mousy little female beside him had to be the gofer no crew could operate without, Reece's included.

But it was the writer-director who drew every eye in the café. Reece's included.

She was laughing at something one of her crew had said. The sound flowed across the room like rich, hot fudge. Her hair looked like chocolate fudge, too, shining and thick and brushed free of the dust and scraggly tangles that had snarled it this morning.

She still wore her boots and baggy fatigue pants. This time, however, she'd paired them with a short-sleeved black top in some clingy material that showed every line and curve of her upper body. The erotic image Reece had conjured up of her earlier popped instantly into his mind. To his disgust, he couldn't quash the startlingly erotic picture as easily as he had before.

He wasn't the only one whose thoughts had focused on Sydney. Arlene Chavez sat with both hands folded into fists in her lap, her lips white at the corners as she took in the director's laughing vitality. Her husband, too, had his eyes locked on the striking brunette.

"Well, well, little Syd's all grown-up."

Jamie's murmur was almost lost in the boisterous group's arrival. Reece caught it, though. So did Arlene. Her gaze wrenched away from the newcomers, and her face filled with such anguish that Reece's heart contracted.

Dammit! Couldn't Chavez see his wife's pain and insecurity?

Evidently not. The man's eyes lit with a gleam that was part predatory and wholly admiring. Tossing his paper napkin onto the table, Jamie rose and strolled forward to intercept the group.

"Sydney?"

"Yes?"

She turned with a look of inquiry that jolted into surprise. Surprise flowed almost instantly into a polite greeting.

"Hello, Jamie."

He took the hand she offered in both of his. "It's been a long time."

"Yes, it has." She freed her hand, eyeing him with the slanting assessment of a person who made her living in the visual arts. "You haven't changed much."

It could have been meant as a compliment or a condemnation. Jamie chose to grin and turn her words back on her.

"You have."

"I'm glad you recognize that fact."

"I heard you almost drove off a cliff last night."

She shook her head, half amused, half exasperated. "Things always did get around fast in this town."

"I'm just glad you weren't hurt." His grin faded. "I also heard your father died. I'm sorry, Syd. He was a good man."

From where Reece sat, it was impossible to miss the change that came over her. She seemed to soften around the edges. Her green eyes grew luminous, her full mouth curved with a genuine warmth.

"Yes, he was."

They shared a small silence, two people bound by the memory of someone they'd both known.

Arlene broke the moment. Rising abruptly with a jerky movement that rattled the glasses and cutlery on the table, she crossed the room to slip her hand into the crook of her husband's arm.

"Is this the famous Sydney Scott I've heard so much about? Why don't you introduce us, darling?"

"This is the one," Jamie replied with unruffled charm. "Arlene, meet Sydney. Syd, this is my wife, Arlene."

Reece wondered how the moviemaker would handle the awkward situation. So did everyone else in the café. Lula had both elbows on the service window behind the counter, her brown eyes wide. A few of the other local patrons whispered and nudged and nodded in the direction of the threesome. Even the noisy crew Sydney had come in with picked up on the buzz and turned curious eyes on their boss.

To her credit she gave the other woman an easy

smile. "I don't know about the famous part, but I am Sydney. It's a pleasure to meet you."

Arlene couldn't let it go there. With her arm still tucked in her husband's, she knifed right to the heart of the matter. "I understand you and my husband were once, shall we say, close friends."

A hush fell over the café. Sydney's ripple of laughter filled the void. "I made a fool of myself over him, you mean. I suppose most girls go through that gawky, hopelessly romantic stage. Thankfully we grow out of it sooner or later."

"Do we?"

"Well, I did, anyway." Her gaze flickered to the fingers Arlene had dug into Jamie's arm. She gentled her voice, as if understanding the woman's need for reassurance. "A long time ago."

Reece stiffened. That was exactly the wrong thing to say around a man like Jamie Chavez. Reece had only met the younger Chavez a few times, but he'd worked with enough men to recognize the type. Handsome, wealthy, restless, chafing a little at having to work with and for his father, despite the fact that he would inherit the vast Chavez ranching and timber empire someday.

That much had been apparent to Reece a few months ago, the night Sebastian Chavez had invited him out to the ranch for drinks and a discussion of the pending dam-repair project. Chavez doted on his only son. He'd displayed a wall of glass cases filled with Jamie's sports trophies and bragged about his keen competitive spirit in both school and business. The bighorn sheep and mountain cat trophies mounted on the den walls, all bagged by Jamie, also indicated someone who loved the thrill of the hunt.

And now a woman who admitted to having made a fool of herself over him laughingly claimed she'd grown out of the infatuation years ago. If Reece had been a betting man, he'd put money on the odds that Jamie would shake loose from his wife's hold... which he did. And that he'd make a move on Sydney...which he now tried to do.

"Not much changes around Chalo Canyon, Syd, even in ten years, but I'd be glad to take you up in my chopper and let you reacquaint yourself with the area. Maybe you can get some shots of the ruins from the air for your documentary."

"I don't think your father would appreciate that, Jamie. He specifically denied me and my crew access to the canyon rim through his land."

Disgusted, Reece lifted his beer. Nothing like telling the man that his daddy was the one calling the shots around here. Didn't she realize that was like waving a red flag in front of a young bull?

His arm froze with the bottle halfway to his mouth. Maybe she did. Maybe she knew exactly what she was doing.

Dammit, he'd wanted to believe her this morning when she'd said she'd come back to Chalo Canyon for one reason only. Now...

"I chopper my own aircraft," Jamie said with a tight smile. "I take up who I want, when I want, where I want."

"Thanks for the offer, but I don't need aerial shots. Or access through Chavez land. I've made other arrangements."

The wrenching heartbreak on Arlene's face as she listened to the byplay between her husband and the moviemaker brought Reece out of his chair. Her expression reminded him so much of his mother's anguish that dark February night. He was still telling himself he was a fool to get involved when he joined the small group.

"Speaking of arrangements, we agreed to get together tonight, remember?"

He kept the words casual, but the lazy glint in his eyes when he looked down at Sydney implied they'd agreed to get together to talk about more than arrangements. To reinforce the impression, Reece aimed a smile her way.

After the first, startled glance, Sydney picked up on his cue. "So we did. Shall we make it your room or mine?" she purred, sliding an arm around his waist.

Whoa! When the woman threw herself into a role, she pulled out all the stops. Reece had to clear his throat before he could push out an answer.

"Mine. I'll clean up while you grab something to eat with your crew."

"I'm not hungry. I just came in with the gang for the company. I'll go with you now. Arlene, maybe we'll get a chance to chat some other time. Jamie…"

Watched avidly by everyone in the café, she searched for a dignified exit line. Once again, Reece stepped into the breech.

"See you around, Chavez."

With a nod to her crew, Sydney preceded Reece out of the café. Neither one of them spoke as they walked through the heat that was rapidly fading to a sweat-cooling seventy or so degrees as dusk turned the sky purple.

Their footsteps crunched on the gravel walkway. Bugs buzzed the glowing yellow bulbs that hung over the row of motel doors. Sydney halted in front of Number Six. Drawing in a long breath, she turned to face him.

"I don't want to sound ungrateful, but I really didn't need rescuing this time."

"What makes you think I stepped in to rescue you?"

"Then who…? Oh. Arlene?"

"Right. Arlene. She doesn't appear to share your confidence that what happened between you and Jamie is, how did you put it? Water over the dam?"

"I can't help what she believes." She hooked her thumbs in the waistband of her baggy pants, her movements stiff and defensive in the lamplight. "I came here to make a movie, and only to make a movie."

"A lot of people seem to believe otherwise."

"Tough. I can't avoid the past, but I'm certainly not going to let it get in my way."

"The past being Jamie Chavez, or his wife?"

Her chin angled. "Look, this isn't really any of your business. Let's just—"

She broke off, her glance darting past him. Behind him, Reece heard the sound of the café door banging shut.

"Oh, hell!"

It didn't take an Einstein to guess who had just walked out. After a short, pregnant pause, Sydney shot him a challenge.

"Okay, hotshot," she muttered, lifting her arms to lock them around his neck. "You scripted this scene. We might as well act it out."

Reece would have had to be poured from reinforced concrete not to respond to the body pressed so seductively against his. As slender as Sydney was, she fit him perfectly in every spot that mattered...and at this point that was just about everywhere. Little sparks ignited where their knees brushed, their hips met, their chests touched.

"Let's make it look good," she whispered, rising up on tiptoe to brush her mouth to his.

Reece held out for all of ten seconds before he lost the short, fierce battle he waged with himself. Her mouth was too soft, too seductive, to ignore. Spanning her waist, he slid his hands around to the small of her back.

She curved inward at the pressure, and the sparks sizzling where their bodies touched burst into flames. Reece shifted, widening his stance, bringing her into the notch between his legs.

She drew back, gasping a little at the intimate contact. The glow from the yellow lightbulb illuminated her startled face. The thrill that zinged through Reece at the sight of her parted lips and flushed face annoyed the hell out of him...and sent a rush of heat straight to his gut.

"Are they still there?" he growled softly.

She dragged her gaze from his to peer around his shoulder. "Yes."

"Guess we'd better do a retake."

With a small smile he bent her backward over his arm.

Chapter 4

When Sydney came up for air, her coherent first thought was that Reece Henderson had chosen the wrong profession. If he performed like this on stage or film, he'd walk away with a fistful of Oscars and Emmys.

The second, far-more-disconcerting thought was that she'd forgotten he was acting about halfway through their bone-rattling kiss.

The crunch of car tires on gravel brought her thumping back to earth. She pushed out of Reece's arms, shaken to the toes of her scuffed boots, just in time to see a silver and maroon utility vehicle with the Chavez Ranch logo on the door pull out of the parking lot. Blowing a shaky breath, she turned back to her co-conspirator.

"That was quite a performance, Mr. Henderson. Let's hope it doesn't get back to your wife."

"I'm not married."

"Engaged? Not that I'm really interested, you understand, but I already have something of a reputation in this town. It would be nice to know what I'm adding to it."

He shoved a hand through his closely trimmed black hair. Sydney felt a little dart of wholly feminine satisfaction at the red that singed his cheeks. She wasn't the only one who'd put more than she planned into the kiss…or taken more out of it.

"No fiancée, no significant other, not even a dog," he replied shortly. "My job keeps me on the road too much for anything that requires a commitment."

Was that a warning? Sydney wondered. Well, she didn't need it. She didn't require anything from Reece Henderson except his cooperation for her documentary.

"Well, that's a relief," she replied dryly. "I don't think I've got room on my chest for another scarlet *A*."

His deliberate glance at the portion of her anatomy under discussion had Sydney battling the absurd urge to cross her arms. She never wore a bra…one, because she wasn't well-enough endowed to require support and two, because she didn't like any unnecessary constriction when she was working. Right now, though, she would gladly have traded a little constriction for the shield of a Maidenform. The tingling at the center of her breasts told her she was showing the effects of that stunning kiss. That, and the way Reece's gaze lingered on her chest.

How embarrassing! And ridiculous! She hadn't allowed any man to fluster her like this since—

Since Jamie.

The memory of her idiocy that long-ago summer acted like a bucket of cold water, fizzling out the shivery feeling left by Reece's mouth and hands and appraising glance. She slanted her head, studying his square chin and faintly disapproving eyes.

"When you stepped into the fray tonight and hinted at something more than a casual acquaintance between us, you obviously wanted to send Jamie Chavez a message. Just out of curiosity, why does it matter to you what either he or his wife thinks?"

His jaw squared. "Maybe I don't like to see a wife humiliated by her husband's interest in another woman."

The barb was directed at her as much as at Jamie. Sydney stiffened, but bit back a sharp reply. She refused to defend herself to him...or anyone else... again.

"And maybe it's because I've got a job to do here," he continued. "I made several trips to Chalo Canyon earlier this year to lay the groundwork and gain the cooperation of the locals, including the Chavez family."

"Sebastian Chavez being the most important and influential of those locals?"

"Exactly. Until he learned about your plans to film the ruins, he was willing to work with me to address the worries of the other ranchers and farmers and businessmen. Since then, he's become a major—"

"Pain in the butt?" Sydney supplied with syrupy sweetness.

"A major opponent of any delay."

"Then he doesn't have anything to worry about,

does he? I'm as anxious to complete my project as you are yours. Speaking of which, are we still on schedule for 9:24 tomorrow?''

''Nine twenty-three,'' he corrected with a disconcerting glint in his blue eyes.

Good Lord! Was that a glimmer of amusement? The idea that Reece Henderson could laugh at himself threw Sydney almost as much as his kiss had. What a contradictory man he was, all disapproving and square-jawed one moment, almost human and too damned attractive for her peace of mind the next.

Good thing her work would keep her occupied from dawn to dusk for the next two weeks. The last thing she needed at this critical juncture was distraction. This project meant too much to her emotionally and financially to jeopardize it with even a mild flirtation.

''I want to position my crew on the east rim just after dawn,'' she said crisply. ''We'll probably shoot most of the day and into the evening, if the light holds. Any problems with that?''

''No. Just check in with me when you leave the area.''

Nodding, she swung around to head back to the café. She'd better remind Zack to curtail his night-owl TV watching or it would take a stick of dynamite to roust him before dawn tomorrow.

''Sydney...''

''Yes?''

He hesitated, then curled that wicked, wonderful mouth into a real-live smile.

''Steer clear of falling rocks.''

''I will.''

She'd steer clear of falling rocks and former lovers and too-handsome engineers. In fact, she swore silently as she reached for the café's screened door, she'd go out of her way to avoid any and all possible distractions until she finished the shoot and shook the dust of Chalo Canyon from her heels forever.

Unfortunately, avoiding distractions and interruptions was easier planned than done.

The predawn sky still wore a mantle of darkness sprinkled with stars when Sydney walked out of her room, laden with one of Tish's camera bags and a backpack filled with water bottles. She'd taken only a step toward the parked van when bright headlights stabbed through the quiet of the sleeping town.

Sydney glanced curiously at the vehicle as it pulled into the motel parking lot. She caught a brief glimpse of the silver Diamond-C logo on its side door before the utility vehicle squealed to a stop a few yards away. Her stomach knotted when she saw that the man at the wheel wasn't Jamie Chavez, but his father.

Okay, girl, she told herself bracingly. You knew this confrontation had to come sooner or later.

Yeah, herself answered, but we were hoping for later.

Come on! Get a grip here. You're not the same easy mark you were the last time you faced Sebastian Chavez.

At nineteen, she'd been shamed to her core by Jamie's father. At twenty-nine, Sydney had cradled her own father's hand while he died a slow, agonizing death. The experience put all else in perspective.

For that reason she was able to greet Jamie's father with a calm nod.

"Hello, Sebastian."

He slammed the door of the utility, a tall man made aristocratic by fine-boned Hispanic features and rigidly erect carriage. The old man never bent, Jamie had once told Sydney with laughing chagrin. He'd break in two before he yielded so much as an inch of his land or his pride.

Or his son.

Even in the darkness, Sydney could see the disdain in his black eyes. The predawn breeze ruffled his silvery hair as he stared at her coldly.

"You've come back."

Sydney confirmed the obvious with a little nod of her head. "Yes."

"You're not welcome in Chalo Canyon."

"I didn't expect a welcome, Sebastian. Not from you."

Nor had she expected the virulent letters he'd written her financial backers when he learned of her proposed documentary. Chavez had done everything in his power to destroy her credibility, her reputation, and her project. Such hatred...or was it reawakened fear that she would take his son from him? Sydney had no patience with or sympathy for either.

"Did you drive into town this early just to make sure I knew I wasn't welcome?"

His head went back. Regal, scornful, he stared down his nose, taking in her ball cap, her ponytail, the worn navy blue sweatshirt she'd pulled on over her tank top to ward off the early-morning chill.

"Never mind. Just load the lunches, will you? I'll roust Tish and the others. I want to get moving."

What she wanted was to get her crew in place. To position her cameras and lose herself in the past once again. She ached to feel that secret, soaring thrill as the mystical village slowly emerged from its decade-long sleep. She *needed* to feel it, needed to share the magic with her father a final time. Her heart thumping in anticipation, she strode back to the open doorways of the rooms beside hers.

Statuesque, six-foot Tish strolled out first, her ebony skin a dark shadow in the predawn. Slightly overweight and fastidious to the point of prissiness, Albert followed a moment later.

"Let's get this show on the road!" Sydney urged. "If our senior engineer's calculations are correct, we need to be in place by seven and have the cameras rolling by eight. Tish, are you ready? Albert? Katie?"

It took another ten minutes to locate the infrared lens Tish had stashed under her bed for safekeeping and five more for Katie and Albert to load the sound console. They wouldn't synthesize sound tracks today, only record them, but Albert preferred to hear the input coming in over the four wireless mikes as he got it, which meant loading up every piece of his equipment every day.

Sydney didn't spare a thought to the physical labor it took to haul the equipment in and out of the motel. With a single camera lens costing upward of five to six thousand dollars, no professional would leave his gear sitting in a van all night, even in a sleepy little town like Chalo Canyon.

Faint streaks of purplish pink hazed the horizon by the time she had both crew and equipment loaded and ready to roll.

"Tish, you ride with me, and we'll talk about settings on the way to the canyon. Zack, you've got the keys to the van?"

"Got 'em." Her assistant ambled to the rented vehicle, his battery-operated Nike shoes flashing. "We'll be right behind you. Just don't drive off any more cliffs, dude-ess."

They made it to the barriers Reece's crew had erected across the canyon rim road just as the eastern sky had begun to glow a reddish gold. In a fever of impatience now, Sydney hustled her crew out of the vehicles and loaded them up for the trek to the vantage point she'd scouted out. As she edged her way around the narrow curve where she'd gone over the cliff, she shot a fond glance toward the piñon where she'd spent the previous night. Once beyond the narrow neck, her boots ate up the dirt track.

Albert was huffing and Zack complaining loudly by the time they reached the point opposite the sunken village. Quiet, mousy Kate went right to work, unpacking sound equipment, spare batteries, videotapes.

Zack flopped down on the ground, arms and legs spread. "Why did I ever throw my lot in with a documentarian?" he grumbled. "I could, like, go to work for Disney and just sit on my butt all day drawing cartoons.

Sydney paid no attention to his grousing. She'd worked with every person on this crew before and knew their strengths and weaknesses. Tish and Albert ranked right up there among the best in the business. Zack... Well, Zack was Zack.

"Okay," she said briskly, "let's go over the shooting script." She knew it almost by heart, but another review wouldn't hurt.

"We'll start with a few wide angles. Tish, as soon as you've got enough light, pan the canyon. I want to convey a sense of its size and scope. I'm also looking for contrasts—dark shadows on red sandstone, the round arch of the cave against the flat cliff face."

"You want contrasts, you'll get contrasts," Tish said confidently, tucking her copy of the shoot script into the pocket of her twill vest. With the loving care of a mother handling a newborn infant, she lifted a long, sausagelike lens out of its case.

"Albert, get me morning sounds. Lots of them. Birds, squirrels, the breeze in the trees. Lazy, sleepy, just coming to life. Let's try for a sense of the world greeting the dawn."

"What you want is your Brigadoon coming awake after its hundred-year sleep."

"Exactly. That's the mood I'm after. A slow awakening. A gentle rebirth. The village slowly emerging from the waters into the sun."

Excitement pulsed along Sydney's nerves, tripping little bursts of energy. This was what she did best. This was what she thrived on. Most people outside the film community thought a documentary simply recorded events as they unfolded. Few realized that a skilled director shaped and shaded the recording to put his or her own artistic interpretation on the footage.

"The next sequence will be the actual emergence. I want a wide-angle shot of the cliff face on camera one, medium close-ups of the village as it clears the water on camera two. As soon as we spot the tower, we'll go maximum zoom. I want to see the stones, the bricks, the empty windows, as they clear the water."

"Got it," Tish said calmly.

"Albert, can you drop one of the mikes to catch some water sounds? Waves lapping against rock, maybe, or a trickle of water running down stone? I know we planned to catch that later, but it would help set the mood..."

The soundman edged to the canyon rim and peered into the dimness below. "How far down is it to the water?"

"More than two hundred feet by now."

"We can try a fishing expedition, but I'm not guaranteeing anything," he said dubiously. "Katie, get that extra roll of cable, will you?"

While her crew set up, Sydney went about her own tasks with a sort of schizophrenic precision. The director in her consulted with Tish on camera placement, studied the light meters that recorded the glow of dawn, listened to the faint whistle of wind magnified through Albert's earphones. All the while her heart pounded and her anxious eyes watched the water level on the opposite cliff face.

Gnawing on her lower lip, she paced the rim. The water inched lower and lower. The sky behind her lightened to purple. The sun rose in a majestic golden ball, painting the cliffs across the shrunken reservoir a rosy pink. The water shaded to gray, then green.

"I'm panning the canyon now," Tish advised, her hand sure and steady on the tripod's handle.

Sydney crowded as close to the camera operator as she could without jostling either her or the equipment. Closing one eye, she followed the camera's tiny video screen as Tish moved it in a slow sweep.

A lump formed right in the middle of her throat. The vast panorama of Chalo Canyon waking to the dawn was magnificent, even framed in a one-inch screen. Light washed down the sandstone cliffs, painting them a rich umber. The same morning sunshine outlined the sharp stone projections and threw the recesses behind them into even starker shadow. Above the cliffs, the sky blued. Below, the waters retreated.

The sun rose higher, clearing the mountains behind them. With agonizing slowness, the shadows on the cliffs across the canyon separated. Distinct, black streaks appeared on the wall of stone.

"There they are," Tish murmured. "The smoke marks left by the cook fires."

Sydney eased away from the camera, her heart pounding. Tish knew what to do. They'd talked about it, planned it. She'd keep one camera trained on those black streaks, follow them down, wait for the village below to appear.

It was close now, so close.

"I'd better change cassettes," Tish murmured. "I don't want both cameras to run out at the same time. You'll skin me alive if I miss this."

Swiftly, Tish ejected the thirty-minute Betacam cassette in camera one and substituted a fresh videotape. She could have used a sixty-minute cassette, or even one that ran for two hours. Neither she nor Sydney wanted to exchange quantity for quality, however.

"Better pull out another battery, too," Sydney murmured to Katie.

The grip nodded and rooted in one of the cases for another spare. Then a quiet settled over the crew as they waited for the village to show itself.

Finally it appeared. First, a rounded arch aged by centuries of smoke. Then a shallow depression. The top of a stone tower. A square window in the stone.

"In close," Sydney whispered to Tish. "As close as you can get. Find me a face in that window."

Without taking her eye from the viewfinder, the camera operator smiled. "This *is* only a legend we're documenting, right, Syd?"

"All myths and legends spring from some aspect of real life," she murmured. "They're tied to the cycles of the season, or a woman's passion for her mate, or the birth of a child."

Sydney hugged her arms. This particular legend was tied to more than just the cycles of the season. It was tied to her youth, her coming of age. And to her father. Especially to her father.

Only when a cloud drifted across the sun and momentarily plunged the canyon into darkness again did she remember that the legend of the Weeping Woman of Chalo Canyon also had its roots in death.

Chapter 5

Sydney got in one glorious day and one moonlit night of shooting before a wall of black clouds rolled in. She awoke before dawn on Wednesday morning to the buzz of her travel alarm and the distant rumble of thunder.

Groping for the alarm, she hit the snooze button and buried her face in the pillow. A moment or two later, the significance of the sounds that had awakened her sunk in. She jerked her head up and stared at the curtained window.

"Oh, no!"

Throwing aside the blanket, she wove her way through stacks of equipment she and the crew had brought into the rooms last night for safekeeping. A quick yank untangled her sleepshirt enough to cover her hot-pink bikini panties. Semidecent, she parted the curtains and peeked outside.

Rain sheeted the window, blurring the darkness beyond. Dismayed, Sydney stared at the puddles of light made by the bulbs hanging above the motel doors. Suddenly a streak of lightning zapped out of the sky and lit everything in greenish-white light.

"Yikes!"

She jumped back and yanked the curtains shut in the foolish belief they would keep out the sizzling electricity. She'd seen enough of these high-desert storms in the years she'd lived in Chalo Canyon to have a healthy respect for them.

Scurrying away from the window, she switched on the bedside lamp and dug her schedule out of the canvas briefcase Zack had scrounged as a replacement for the one that now resided at the bottom of the gorge. With legs crossed under her, she studied the schedule.

The crew had arrived on Monday and got in some good footage around the canyon rim. Yesterday, they'd shot the emergence sequence and some good visuals of moonlight playing on the village.

Today, with the reservoir fully emptied, they were scheduled to hike down into the canyon and shoot some close-ins of the ruins. She'd already arranged for a team of locals to haul in the crates containing the ladders and pulleys her crew would need to get themselves and their equipment up to the cave.

Worrying her lower lip with her teeth, Sydney studied her schedule. She'd built in some slippage, but not much. She'd planned on eight good days of shooting. She could live with six. Between trips down to the ruins, she intended to tape interviews with selected local residents to add authenticity and local color to the legend.

And that was the easy part. After the actual shoot would come months of work in her L.A. studio, editing the tapes, synthesizing sound tracks, recording the scripted narrative, adding the titles and graphics that transformed raw footage into a stunning visual statement. If all went as planned, she would finish the first cut by the end of August and the fine cut by mid-September. PBS wanted to view the edited master tape by October fifteenth. Once approved, the documentary would broadcast in the spring, which allowed plenty of time to get it in the running for next year's Oscars.

Another nomination would go a long way toward helping her pay off the loan for her studio. Even more important, completing this project would fulfill her promise to her father. She'd put Chalo Canyon and her past behind her once and for all and get on with her life.

Sighing, Sydney slumped back against the rickety headboard. She missed her dad so much. She wasn't lonely, exactly. Her grief had dulled enough for her to accept his loss, and her various projects kept her too busy to indulge in long periods of introspection or sadness. But at moments like this, with the night still wrapping the world in darkness and rolling thunder threatening her with hours of enforced idleness, she felt the emptiness.

There'd been other men besides her father in her life, of course. But after Jamie Chavez, she'd remained wary. Cautious. In retrospect she probably owed Jamie a real debt of gratitude. He'd taught her a valuable lesson, so much so that she'd kept subsequent relationships light and unentangling. None of the men she'd dated over the years had tempted her into anything more than casual companionship.

Then again, none of them had kissed her the way Reece Henderson had.

The memory of those startling moments outside her motel room that night slid into Sydney's mind and wouldn't slide out. To her surprise, a tight little flicker of desire ignited low in her belly.

Frowning, she willed it away. *Forget it, girl! He's not your type, not that you have a clue what your type is. Besides, he's convinced you've only come back to Chalo Canyon to wreak havoc among the natives.*

The reminder of the barely disguised disdain she'd glimpsed in Reece's eyes that night irritated her so much that she shot another glance at the clock. Almost six. He should be up by now.

Jamming the receiver to her ear, she punched in the number for Reece's room. The phone shrilled once, twice, three times. She'd just started to disconnect when he picked up.

"Henderson."

Sydney had to admit the man had a voice like cut velvet. Deep. Rich. Sexy smooth, with just enough of a Southwestern accent to hint at cowboys in old Stetsons and tight jeans. Briefly she wondered if he'd ever considered doing voice-overs to supplement his income. Probably not. She had no idea what engineers earned, but from the way his men jumped every time he opened his mouth, he must rank right up there at the top of the pay scale.

"Reece, it's Sydney."

"Yes?"

"It's raining."

There was a moment of dead silence.

"You called me at 5:46 a.m. to apprise me of that?"

Did the man always think so precisely, for heaven's sake?

"Were you asleep?"

"No, I was in the shower. Now, I'm soaking wet, buck naked, and wondering what the hell you expect me to do about the fact that it's raining."

Sternly, Sydney suppressed a vivid mental image of Reece Henderson soaking wet and buck naked.

"I don't expect you to do anything except give me blanket authority to trek into the canyon when the rain stops."

"Call me when the weather clears. We'll talk about it then."

Her back teeth ground together. "Can't we compromise a little? I've hired a guide and some locals to haul in the ropes and ladders we'll need to get up to the ruins. I hate to waste the whole day if I don't have to. How about at least letting us drive to the access point to wait out the storm?"

"It's not just the rain in this vicinity we have to worry about," he pointed out. "It's been raining north of us, too. I don't want you or your crew caught by a flash flood."

"Neither do I," she assured him earnestly. "One disaster per project is my limit. We'll await your go-ahead before trekking into the canyon."

Another silence followed.

Sydney wasn't above wheedling and cajoling when the occasion demanded. She'd already learned, however, that Reece wasn't particularly wheedlable.

"All right. Call and speak with me personally before you go in."

"Thanks."

She hung up before he could add any further caveats. Dragging up her knees, she looped her arms around them and tried to detail the sights and sounds they would record when they got to the ruins. To her disgust her mind kept zinging back to the vivid and wholly erotic mental image of Reece Henderson's wet buns.

Four rooms away Reece dropped the phone into its cradle and headed back to the shower. He'd been awake for an hour, stretched out in bed, waiting for the lightning to pass before he showered and shaved, thinking about his crew, about the stress fracture, about the exterior-damage assessment he hoped to complete today.

Hell, who was he kidding? He'd spent most of the time trying not to think about Sydney.

He still couldn't quite believe he'd bent her over his arm that night and laid one on her like that. He hadn't experienced such a brainless, idiotic, caveman response to the feel of a woman's body pressed against his since…since…

Since never.

The unpalatable truth stared him in the face, and he didn't much like it. Granted, Sydney Scott could rouse a dead man with those flashing green eyes and supple curves, not to mention the round, neat bottom that had fit so enticingly in Reece's lap, but he'd met his share of enticing women in his time. Once, he'd even thought about marrying one. A brown-eyed Brazilian beauty with a shy smile and a degree in agriculture had kept him in South America long past the time required for the job that had taken him there. She'd shied away from a permanent commitment to a foreigner, however, and Reece had left Brazil with his heart surprisingly undented.

Even then, even with Elena, he'd never felt such a hard, tight slam of lust when he'd taken her in his arms. He'd wanted her, yes, but with a controlled passion, a measured need...totally unlike the urgency that knifed through him when Sydney plastered herself against his chest.

Frowning, Reece turned his face up to the tepid water. Of all the rowdy Henderson brothers, he'd always exercised the most self-discipline in his work, in his finances, in his personal habits. He enjoyed a good fight, sure, and had been known to down his share of brews with his brothers, although the last time any of them had gotten drunk, really, honest-to-goodness, falling down drunk, was just after Jake's high school graduation. All five of them, even eight-year-old Sam, had sneaked off to one of the line shacks with a couple of cases of beer to celebrate Jake's passage into manhood. Their father had found them the next morning and never said a word about their pasty faces and red-veined eyes.

At the thought of his father, Reece stiffened. He still couldn't think of Big John without a tight whip of anger. The fact that the old man had cheated on his wife was bad enough. Leaving those damned let-

ters behind for her to find just when her grief had
started to heal made his betrayal even worse.

Reece didn't have any use for a man who would
betray his wife. Or for the woman who'd encourage
him to do it...which brought his thoughts back full
circle to Sydney.

Why had she gone along with Reece's clumsy attempt to save Arlene embarrassment? To discourage
Jamie? Or dig the spur in deeper? Make him think
he had a rival? Rouse his competitive instincts even
more?

Looking back on it, Reece found himself wanting
to believe her dry comment that it was all water over
the dam. He'd supervised enough men and women
over the years to trust his instincts about people, and
his instincts were telling him to take Sydney at her
word, to accept that she'd returned to Chalo Canyon
to make a movie.

Or maybe he just wanted to believe her...because
he wanted *her*.

Ducking his head under the pulsing stream, he
soaped his scalp. Why didn't he just admit the
woman had a mouth made for sin and leave it at that?
He didn't have time for any more quixotic gestures
or clumsy attempts to salvage anyone's pride, let
alone for lusty little interludes with the delectable
Ms. Scott.

Comfortable in a blue workshirt, jeans, sturdy
boots and his trusty Stetson, he left his room twenty
minutes later and joined the men hunched over mugs
of coffee and platters of *huevos rancheros* in the res-
taurant. The accommodating Lula provided the crew
with thermoses of steaming coffee to sustain them

during the drive to the dam. Headlights on, windshield wipers swiping at the rain, the work vehicles formed a small caravan and headed out.

As they pulled out of the parking lot, the light glowing behind the curtains of Unit Six caught Reece's eye. Resolutely, he put Sydney Scott out of his mind.

The pounding rain had fizzled to foggy mist by the time Sydney and her crew began loading their equipment. They had most of it stowed when the guide she'd hired drove up in a pickup covered with more rust than paint.

A bubble of delight danced through her veins when Henry Three Pines stepped out of the vehicle. She remembered him from the times he and her father worked together—her dad as fish and game warden, Henry as headman of the Hopi clan whose lands bordered the Chalo River Reservoir. Sydney had talked to him again by phone a few months ago. He'd agreed to act as their guide and, she hoped, share some of the lore of the Anasazi who'd inhabited the region.

She had no idea how old he was. He'd seemed as ancient as the earth two decades ago. Now his immense dignity and the sheer visual magic of his weathered face, shadowed by a brown felt hat with rattlesnake skin band, called to the filmmaker in her.

"Henry! It's good to see you again."

"And you, Little Squirrel."

Sydney grinned at the nickname he'd given the pesky, curious, irrepressible nine-year-old who'd dogged his heels her first summer in Chalo Canyon.

His gnarled hands folded over hers. His black eyes spoke to the little knot of pain she carried just under her heart.

"I know you still sorrow for your father, but he lives on in spirit with the kachina."

As an outsider, Sydney made no claim to understanding the complicated and all-pervasive religious structure the Hopi had evolved over the centuries. She knew only that it answered the insecurities of a people living in a harsh environment. She still treasured the hand-carved wooden kachina doll Henry had presented her upon her departure from Chalo Canyon, and took comfort from the understanding in his seamed face.

"He is why you've come back," Henry said softly. "You wish to honor him with this film you make."

"Yes."

"It is good for a daughter to honor her father." His arthritic hands squeezed gently. "It is good for me to help her do so."

"Thank you."

His calm gaze took in the assembled crew. He greeted each of them with grave courtesy, awing even the still-sleepy Zack into a handshake instead of his customary high five.

"Hey, dude, er, Mr. Three Pines, er, sir."

"Call me Henry." He turned back to Sydney, his aged face unflappable. "I am told you hired men to deliver crates to the canyon."

"I did." Frowning, she swiped a look at her watch. "They should have been here by now."

"They do not come."

"What?"

"Sebastian Chavez has told them they must not aid you."

Her jaw sprang shut, effectively stopping a curse.

"If you wish," Henry said calmly, "I'll arrange for my grandsons to carry these crates down into the canyon. They've gone to Phoenix this morning to enroll at the university for the fall semester, but they return later this afternoon."

Swiftly Sydney reordered the shoot schedule. *If* the rain let up, and *if* Reece gave them permission to trek down into the canyon, they could concentrate on more background shots until Henry's grandsons arrived with the heavy equipment. Almost choking with disappointment that she'd have to wait to get into the ruins, she accepted Henry's offer.

With Zack driving the van, Sydney and Henry climbed into the replacement Blazer. This one, thank goodness, came equipped with automatic drive. She didn't even *want* to think about working a clutch on narrow, wet roads.

Denied direct access to the western rim through Sebastian Chavez's property, they had to drive a good twenty miles out of their way. Sydney seethed for a good part of the way over Sebastian's attempts to block her shoot.

Well, no amount of contrariness on his part was going to drive her away. Not this time.

They crossed the river via a bridge south of the dam, then headed north. A few miles later the asphalt road dwindled to an unimproved dirt track. By the time their small caravan reached the narrow path that wound down into the canyon, the rainy mist had begun to dissipate.

Sydney had just picked up her cell phone to check in with Reece when Tish jumped out of the van with an ecstatic shout.

"Omigod, look at that!"

The whole crew froze as the mists parted, revealing a perfect, shimmering rainbow. One end disappeared in the clouds to the east. The other touched down right above the distant cliffs that sheltered the ruins.

Tish dived back into the van, all six feet of her ablaze with excitement. Swooping up one of the video cameras, she darted toward the canyon rim.

With her own swan dive over the cliffs still fresh in her memory, Sydney hotfooted after the camera operator and grabbed the tail of her tan safari shirt. A swift tug yanked her back.

"Not so close to the edge."

The statuesque woman shuffled backward, her eye already glued to the view finder. "Katie! Get the fish-eye lens! No, no, the EF 15! Dammit, where's my tripod?"

"I've got it!" Zack yelled.

Whipping out the telescoping legs, he set the tripod up for her while Katie passed her the wide-angle lens. Within mere seconds, Tish had the camera stabilized and trained on the shimmering rainbow.

Only then did Sydney notice Henry Three Pines standing apart from all the bustle, his gaze trained on the distant arc of color. A faint memory of ancient lore pinged in Sydney's mind, something about the spirits residing half the year in Hopi villages, then using rainbows as a bridge when they returned to their underground dwelling places for the rest of the year.

"Albert," she murmured. "Give me a hand mike and get ready for a take."

She approached slowly, respectfully. She wouldn't intrude if Henry wanted solitude, nor would she violate his religious beliefs by capturing his image on video. But if he wished to share the legend, she wanted it on tape.

"Will you speak to me of rainbows?" she asked softly.

He smiled, his face folding into a thousand tiny lines. "Yes, Squirrel, I will speak to you of rainbows."

She held her breath, mesmerized by his voice, by his tales of the spirits, of the elemental fusing of earth and sky. Her own spirits soared with the beauty of the moment.

The rainbow dissolved ten minutes later, leaving Sydney filled with the satisfaction of a good take. What started out as a dreary morning had just yielded an unexpected bonus. Now if only Reece Henderson would give them the okay to trek down into the canyon....

He did. Grudgingly. "Just keep the phone with you at all times."

"I will."

"Let me know when you leave the area."

She had to strain to hear him. The signal kept cutting in and out. She'd better get Zack to dig out the extra battery pack.

"And watch out for snakes."

"Trust me, I'll definitely do that!"

On fire with anticipation, she snapped the cell phone shut, helped her crew load their essential supplies into backpacks and fell in line behind Henry as he picked his way down into the canyon.

The sun came out before they were halfway down. By the time they reached the canyon floor and the banks of the Chalo River, the mists had burned away, and the heat rose in shimmering waves from the limestone.

Throughout the descent, Sydney had the eerie sensation of climbing down to an ocean bottom. Her lively imagination couldn't help likening the experience to what the Israelites must have felt when Moses parted the Red Sea and led them into its cavernous depths.

After ten years underwater, the dark canyon walls gave off a dank smell. Silvery gray lichenlike plant forms made its sandstone slopes treacherous. The cottonwoods that had grown along the riverbank before the dam's construction still remained, their branches stripped of all green.

And it was quiet, unearthly still, without any birds or scurrying desert creatures or even the rustle of wind through the leaves. In fact, there were no leaves or greenery of any kind below the canyon rim. The trees had drowned long ago. Now, their blackened trunks and naked limbs were starkly silhouetted against the sky. The only sound that disturbed the stillness was the river's murmur.

Sweating and red-faced, the crew regrouped at the riverbank. Tugging off his Australian bush cap, Albert waved it in front of his face to stir some air.

"How far to the cave?" he asked.

"Half a mile as the crow flies. A mile as the river flows."

The portly soundman gulped and beat the air with his hat.

"You okay?" Sydney asked quietly, concerned by the red flush heating his face.

"Yeah. Just a little out of shape."

"We'll rest here for a while."

"No, let's go on."

A professional down to the tips of his designer, ostrich-skin boots, Albert would keel over in a dead faint before he caused a schedule slip. That was one of the reasons Sydney had hired him for this project, and one of the reasons she watched him closely as Henry led them along the riverbed for another mile.

The narrow gorge gradually widened. The river also widened and became more shallow, bordered by a wide ledge of sandstone. Finally the small party stood below the cave that housed the cliff dwellings. Necks craned, they stared up at the wet, glistening ruins. Tish was the first one to break the silence.

"The Anasazi must have been part monkey to climb up and down these cliffs every day."

Sydney had researched the ancient peoples thoroughly as part of her prep work for the shoot. "They used wooden ladders that they could pull up if attacked," she explained. "Or they climbed down from the canyon rim using those hand- and footholds carved into the rock."

Tilting her head back, the camera operator squinted at the shallow holes carved in the cliff face. A moment later she shook her head.

"You know how much I like working with you, Syd. I didn't object when you decked me out in netting and walked me into that room full of buzzing bees. I didn't like it, but I didn't object. And that time in Peru, when we had to dodge llama doo-doo all during the long climb up to Machu Picchu, did I complain?"

"Yes. Loudly."

"Only when the llama behind me took a nip at my tush," she protested. "But there's no way I'm crawling up that rock wall with all my equipment slung over my back."

"Not to worry," Sydney assured her. "Henry's grandsons will deliver the ropes and pulleys and aluminum ladders we had shipped in later this afternoon. Until they get here, we'll concentrate on exteriors."

She turned a smile at her father's friend.

"And Henry has agreed to tell us of the Ancient Ones who lived here. We'll use his voice for part of the back story narration. So let's get to it, troops. Time and sunlight wait for no man...or woman for that matter."

Within minutes the various members of her crew were hard at it. Sydney, whose background and training had her fingers itching for a camera, forced herself to oversee, to direct, to suggest.

This was the work she loved, and she got into it heart and soul. She thought nothing of squatting in the mud of the riverbank with Tish to study camera angles, climbing halfway up a tree to help Katie hang a mike, or sitting cross-legged beside Henry while an intense, earphoned Albert recorded the old man's tales.

Totally absorbed, Sydney spent the rest of the morning engaged in the craft of weaving dreams into reality. Just past noon the sound of a helicopter shattered the canyon's quiet and brought first Jamie Chavez, then a coldly furious Reece down on her.

Chapter 6

The helo came swooping up the canyon from the south.

Sydney heard it first through earphones. She'd borrowed a set from Albert to listen to the replay of Henry Three Pines' description of the Basket Makers, the earliest of the Ancient Ones to inhabit the canyon. Frowning, she hunched her shoulders and tried to tune out the muffled *whump-whump-whump*.

She couldn't, however, ignore the sudden gust of wind that stirred every piece of paper in the small camp, including her script, the video footage sheets and the loose-leaf pages of notes she'd made of the day's shoot. With a gasp of dismay, she tore off the earphones and lunged for the scattering papers. She managed to catch a handful or two, but the rest swirled and twirled and danced on the now-vicious downdraft. Shouting at Zack and Katie to help, she snatched them out of the air.

Consequently she greeted the pilot who climbed out of the maroon-and-silver helo with something less than civility.

"Thanks a lot! You almost sent my cue sheets and shoot notes flying to the four corners of the canyon."

Jamie blinked, thrown off stride for all of three or four seconds before his charm kicked into gear.

"Sorry 'bout that, Syd."

She planted both hands on her hips, glaring. The roguish grin that had melted her knees ten years ago now had zero effect on her. Less than zero.

"What do you want, Chavez?"

"It's not what *I* want."

His voice dropped, hinted at an intimacy that didn't exist. Never really existed, she knew with the unerring accuracy of twenty-twenty hindsight.

"It's what you want, Syd."

She wasn't in the mood for suggestive innuendoes. "In case I didn't make myself clear last night, I'm not interested in picking up where I left off ten years ago. I came back to Chalo Canyon to make a movie. *Only* to make a movie."

For Pete's sake, how many times did she have to repeat herself? She didn't need this distraction, and she certainly didn't need any more after-hours visits from Sebastian Chavez.

"I'm in the middle of a shoot here, Jamie, which you've just totally disrupted. Why don't you climb back into your little toy and take off?"

"Sure." Unruffled, he torqued his grin up another notch. "Do you want me to leave before or after I unload your crates of equipment?"

Her eyes narrowed. She suspected Sebastian had

no idea Jamie had taken it upon himself to haul in her equipment, and wouldn't like it when he found out about it. Tough! Father and son could work that one out between them. Right now, all she cared about was getting up to the ruins.

"After," she conceded.

"I thought so."

Eager to climb up to the cave, the entire crew pitched in to help Jamie unload two folding aluminum ladders and a large crate containing pulleys and winches. Stripped down to her sleeveless orange tank top and jeans, Sydney helped Zack muscle one ladder into position while Tish and Albert unfolded the other.

They were just about to attack the crates when Reece appeared. He strode along the wide sandstone ledge that formed the river's bank with a sure-footed agility that made a mockery of the far-slower pace Sydney and her crew had managed earlier.

Watching him approach, she felt her heart give a little bump against her ribs. To hell with engineering and building dams. Reece Henderson belonged in Hollywood. That rawhide-smooth voice of his, alone, would earn him a fortune. Paired with his broad shoulders and that lean-hipped, long-legged, outta-my-way stride, he was every woman's fantasy come to life.

Giving in to an impulse that was as natural to her as breathing, Sydney snatched up one of the video cams. She had no idea what she'd do with this footage, but it was too darned good to miss. Framing the man against the red sandstone cliffs, she zoomed in.

Only then did she catch the tight-lipped expression on her subject's face.

Oh-oh. Evidently this wasn't a social visit. Sighing, she lowered the camera.

He joined their little group a moment later. The look he zinged from Jamie to her and back again set Sydney's teeth on edge. She would eat dirt before she defended herself against the scorn on Reece's face, or protest yet again that she had no interest in Jamie Chavez.

"I've been trying to reach you for the past hour," he said tightly. "Where the hell's your phone?"

Bristling, Sydney whipped it out of her pants pocket. "Right here."

Too late she remembered the weak battery. She'd gotten so caught up in the trek down the canyon that she'd forgotten to change it. Biting back a groan, she glanced down at the instrument. Sure enough, the liquid crystal display showed a blank face.

"The battery's dead." Feeling like ten kinds of a fool, she handed it to Zack with quiet instructions to dig out the spare battery.

"I'm sorry," she told Reece, bracing herself for the broadside she expected him to deliver. "I'll make sure that doesn't happen again."

"Do that," he snapped.

She ground her teeth, mentally counting to ten. "Why were you trying to contact me?"

"To verify the report I got of a helo touching down close to the ruins." His icy blue eyes sliced to Jamie, then back to Sydney. "I thought I'd made myself clear that all incursions into the restricted area behind the dam had to be coordinated with me."

She wasn't taking the fall for Jamie Chavez. Not this time.

"You did," she replied coolly. "Very clear."

With a careless shrug, Jamie stepped into the breach. "I thought I'd just help Syd out by delivering her gear. She didn't know I was coming."

"Neither did your father," Reece said shortly.

Jamie stiffened. "You called him?"

"He called me."

From the tight angle to Jamie's jaw, Sydney knew she'd guessed right. Obviously he hadn't told his father about his little excursion to the canyon.

Or his wife, she'd bet.

Her mouth twisted. How in the world had she been so blind ten years ago? How had she let herself fall for a handsome face and a flashing smile, and never spared a thought to the person behind them? She owed Sebastian for opening her eyes. She really did. She'd try to remember that the next time he came down on her with both boots, she thought sardonically.

"Sorry, Henderson," Jamie said with a stiff edge to his voice. "I'm used to doing things my way around here."

"Not this time, Chavez. No more flights into the canyon without my approval."

Jamie's mouth set, and for a moment Sydney wondered if he'd grown enough backbone in the past ten years to challenge the flat order or the man who gave it.

Evidently not. He caved. Ungraciously.

"Yeah, well, I'll give you a call next time I decide to fly in and check on Syd."

"See that you do."

Without her quite knowing how or when it happened, the ground had shifted. The air between the two men took on a charged sensation. Reece made no overt move toward her, as he had at the café the other night, but Jamie seemed to take his challenge personally.

Sydney had the oddest sensation, as if she was an old soup bone tossed down between two sleek, well-fed hounds. Neither one really wanted her, but neither was about to allow the other too near.

"You boys work this out between you," she said with a snap. "I've got work to do."

Jamie left in a whirl of rotor blades and a flash of sunlight on maroon and silver a few minutes later. If not for the downdraft produced by the helo, Sydney wouldn't have noticed his departure. She was on her knees, helping Zack and the others unpack the crate she'd had shipped in from L.A. Henry Three Pines sat in the shade of the canyon wall, conversing comfortably with Reece and drawing deep, satisfied drags on the cheroot the engineer had produced from his shirt pocket.

Zack had just pried open the lid of the first crate when the flush on Albert's face snagged Sydney's attention. She sat back on her heels, instantly contrite. He wasn't used to this blazing Arizona heat. If she'd been thinking of anything except getting up to the ruins, she would've seen how it affected him.

"Why don't you and Katie pack it in for the day?" she suggested casually. "We've got enough sound takes of the river and the canyon. No sense you two sitting around here just waiting for the wind to pick up. Leave me a recorder and a mike just in case, then take the Blazer back to town."

"Well…" Albert mopped his brow, reluctant but obviously considering the offer.

Sydney threw a look over her shoulder. "Maybe Reece will walk you out of the canyon. He knows the way. Hang loose, I'll ask him."

When she put the question to him, the engineer nodded his assent. "Sure."

He speared a look at the tangle of ropes and blocks in the scattered crates, started to say something, then rolled his shoulders in a quick shrug.

"Tell your man…Al, is it?"

"Albert."

"Tell Albert to gather his gear," he said curtly, still obviously less than pleased with her and her dead battery. "I want to get back to the dam."

"Yes, sir!" She flipped him the Hollywood version of a military salute and marched away with a stiff-kneed goose step.

Reece leaned against the cliff face, trying to hold on to his anger. He *wanted* to hold on to it. He'd been stewing ever since the call from Sebastian, and come to a near boil when he'd spotted Jamie Chavez laying his particular brand of charm on a sweat-streaked, tumble-haired, thoroughly seductive Sydney.

Calling himself a fool for almost believing her when she'd protested that she had no interest in Chavez, Jr., he'd wanted to let rip. Only the rigid self-control his brothers had delighted in putting to the test so many times over the years kept his anger tightly leashed.

He had to admit, though, that Sydney didn't seem particularly concerned whether Chavez stayed or left once he unloaded his cargo. She showed far more interest in the crates than in their deliverer, and didn't appear at all distressed by Reece's dictum barring Chavez from any further unauthorized intrusions into the restricted area behind the dam.

Was that part of her game? Was she still playing hard to get? Or did she really not care about Chavez?

The fact that Reece couldn't make up his mind one way or the other annoyed the hell out of him. He tended to see things in black and white. He admitted it. He preferred to keep business and personal matters neat, well-defined, precisely aligned.

Which was why the engineer in him shuddered as he watched Sydney and the green-haired kid pull a tangle of ropes and pulleys out of the crate and dump them carelessly on the ground.

"Funny," the kid—Zack—commented. "This contraption didn't look, you know, so complicated when the guy in L.A. demonstrated it." Huffing, he lifted a clanking block and pulley. "Or so heavy."

"Does it come with instructions?"

"I dunno."

Sydney bent over, delving into the crate for a set of instructions. In the process, she gave Reece a view of a slender, rounded backside that dried the saliva in his mouth and throat. A moment later she sat back down on her heels, dangling a length of rope in one hand. Frustration pulled her lips into a pout as she eyed the tangle of blocks and pulleys.

"I can take a camera apart and clean it faster than a Marine can field strip his M-16, but this stuff…"

She glanced from the ropes to Reece, calculating, debating. He saw what was coming and steeled himself against the reluctant appeal.

"I don't suppose you'd consider giving us the benefit of your expertise on this thing before you go?"

No. No way. He needed to get back to the dam. The computerized stress simulations should be coming off the Cray supercomputer in D.C. within the next hour. He'd already put a dent in his schedule by driving up here.

Ever after, Reece could never decide whether it was the unsightly tangle of rope in Sydney's hand or the sweat streak between her breasts that changed his mind. Somehow, he couldn't stand the thought of her and her crew wrestling with the heavy blocks in this heat…and making a mess of it. Sighing, he told Albert and the mousy gofer to hang loose for a few minutes, and strolled over to join the small group clustered around the crate.

"This 'thing,' as you call it, is one of the oldest machines invented by man."

Calmly, methodically, Reece helped lay the various pieces of the mechanism in orderly rows on the ground.

"Like the fulcrum and the lever, the pulley trades distance for force or force for distance."

Sydney shot the others a look. "Right. Distance for force."

His professional instincts roused now, Reece tried a more basic, textbook explanation.

"Essentially, all machines are force multipliers.

Work equals force multiplied by the distance over which the force acts. Thus, by increasing the distance via a system of block and tackles like this, you increase the mechanical advantage—the ratio of the load-to-overcome versus the effort expended.''

Her face arranged in suitably grave lines, Sydney nodded, but Reece couldn't miss the laughter dancing in her green eyes. His stomach muscles did a little force multiplying of their own.

Dammit! How could she tie him up in knots with a single, sparkling glance?

The reminder that she tied Chavez up in exactly the same way did little to loosen the knots. Thumbs hooked in the belt loops of his jeans, Reece scowled at the array of equipment.

''Unless you're planning to lift steel girders to reinforce the walls of some of those ruins, you've got four times what you'll need here. Block and tackles are only necessary for heavy loads.''

Sydney and Tish turned accusing eyes on the beringed Zack. His skinny shoulders lifted in a defensive shrug.

''Like, I should know that?''

''Well, I guess more is better than not enough,'' Sydney said, bringing those dazzling green eyes back to Reece again. ''If you'll just show us which end of the rope goes where, we'll take it from there.''

He winced. Looked at his watch. Struggled valiantly against an overwhelming urge to see the job done right...and lost. With a resigned sigh, he unbuttoned his shirt and pulled it off. Folding it neatly, he laid it on a nearby rock.

''All right. I'll show you which end goes where.''

Sydney didn't even notice that her lower jaw had dropped until Tish elbowed her in the ribs. Hard.

"Close your mouth, girl. You're sucking in gnats."

She was sucking in more than gnats. She was sucking in the sight of Reece Henderson's wide shoulders, rippling muscles and intriguingly concave belly with that little twirl of silky black hair just above the navel.

Oh, God! Where was her camera? Why couldn't she ever find extras who looked like this when she needed them? Would he let her capture him stripped to the waist like this on video?

The thought brought reality crashing down.

She hadn't put herself in hock, spent the past eight months lining up funding, and hired an outrageously expensive crew to document Reece Henderson's admittedly spectacular bod. She'd made a promise to her father, and to herself in his memory—a promise she intended to get to work on as soon as Reece finished doing whatever he was doing.

It didn't take him long. Ignoring the heavy wooden blocks, he tied two smaller pulleys to a bundle of hinged wooden struts, then looped a length of rope over his head and shoulders.

"I'll climb up to the ledge and drop a line for the bundle."

"I'll go with you," Sydney said quickly.

She beat him to the aluminum ladder by a second or two. She wasn't about to let anyone set foot in the ruins ahead of her. This was her dream, her and her father's. She'd waited ten years for this moment.

Her heart started pounding the instant she set her

foot on the first rung. By the time she swung onto the ledge, it thundered in her ears.

She stood transfixed a few feet from the edge, afraid to move, almost afraid to breathe for fear the ruins would collapse or crumble or otherwise disintegrate before she could explore their secrets. The fear was irrational, she knew. These stone buildings and the people who occupied them had survived hundreds of years under Arizona's blistering sun. After the villagers abandoned their homes and the fields of maize, beans and squash they cultivated on the canyon rim, the deserted village had remained tucked away in this isolated cave for hundreds more. Even decades under water hadn't destroyed them.

Still, Sydney absorbed a sense of ephemeral beauty through every pore of her body. Perhaps the ruins seemed so fragile because they rose from the waters for such a short time, only to sink into oblivion once again when the reservoir filled. Caught up in their spell, she peered through patterns of sunlight on shadow. Above her arched the smoke-blackened roof of the cave. Ahead of her, so close she could touch it, stood a low wall. Hesitantly, tentatively, she reached out. The stone felt cool and dry under her fingertips.

"The cliff dwellers knew what they were doing."

Reece loomed behind her, speaking softly, sounding every bit as awed as Sydney by the ancient ruins.

"They built their homes in cliffs facing east or south to take advantage of solar energy," he murmured. "The morning sun warmed their homes in winter, and the cliffs protected them from the fierce heat of the afternoon sun in summer."

His fingers brushed the same wall Sydney's had.

"Look at this. They chinked the rocks together so tightly the structure held even though the water's eaten away at the mud mixed with straw they used for mortar."

The reverence in his voice brought a smile to her eyes. She didn't know a fulcrum from an inclined plane, but his appreciation for the Ancient Ones' architectural skills she could relate to. Feeling more in harmony with the man than at any other time in their brief acquaintance, she turned to share some of her newly gained knowledge.

The little movement trapped her between the stone wall and Reece's chest. Sydney breathed in his scent, a mixture of hot sun and clean, healthy sweat, and felt her heart do a quick little number against her ribs. If she rose up on tiptoe, if she stretched just a few inches, she could touch her mouth to his.

The idea of drawing him into another of those soul-shattering kisses drove everything, even the ruins, from her mind for a moment or two.

But only a moment or two.

She'd invested too much of herself and her dreams in this project to lose her perspective only seconds after setting foot on the ledge. Recalling herself with a start, she scooted to one side at the precise instant Reece moved the other way, looking every bit as relieved as she at the near miss. With brisk efficiency, he dropped the rope line over the ledge, hauled up the bundle of wooden supports, and set about rigging a simple pulley.

A shout to Tish signaled that the mechanism—correction, the force multiplier—was operational.

Following Reece's instructions, the camera operator and Zack attached a case of equipment.

Resolutely Sydney kept her back turned as Reece hauled up the first load. No sense risking another mouth full of gnats by admiring the way the light played over the sweat glistening on his back, or dwelling on the poetry of his lean, muscled torso in motion.

In less than ten minutes, both her reduced crew and their equipment had gained the cave. Eager to get to work, Zack and Tish dug into the packs.

When Reece dusted his hands on his jeans and prepared to leave, common courtesy dictated that Sydney thank him for his efforts. She even offered to buy him dinner later at the Lone Eagle Café in exchange for his help.

"Some other time, maybe." He swung onto the ladder. "If the data I requested comes in this afternoon, I'll be putting in some long, late nights."

"Sure. See you around, then."

As brush-offs went, it was relatively benign. Nothing like the humiliation Sydney had experienced at Jamie Chavez's hands ten years ago.

Yet for some reason, Reece Henderson's rugged features and casual dismissal of her offer disrupted her thoughts far more than they should have in the hours that followed.

Chapter 7

Sebastian didn't confront his son about his flight into the canyon until the following afternoon. He wanted to remain calm and approach the matter of Sydney Scott rationally, but his distress went too deep...and his fear. Five minutes into the discussion, his cheekbones were singed with red.

"I won't have it!"

He stood ramrod straight, facing his son across the oak trestle table that served as his desk.

"This woman almost destroyed all your plans and dreams ten years ago. You can't allow her to do so again. *I* can't allow it."

"My plans and dreams?" As stiff and unyielding as his father, Jamie gave a huff of derision. "Your plans, you mean. For me. For Arlene. For the convenient joining of your lands with my wife's."

Sebastian reared back, stung. "I wanted only your

happiness. That's all I've ever wanted. Since the day your mother…''

His throat worked. Even after all these years, he couldn't speak of his young wife's treachery without tasting bitter gall.

''Since the day your mother went away, I've lived my life for you.''

Jamie blew out a long breath. Despite their occasional arguments, neither father nor son ever denied the bond between them. As his belligerence drained, however, guilt took its place. He felt so damned suffocated by his father's all-consuming love, so trapped.

''Yes, I know you have.''

Like a hawk, his father moved in to take advantage of his weakening. ''Sydney Scott came back to Chalo Canyon to take her revenge on us. You can't trust her.''

''No, Dad. *You* can't trust her, any more than you've trusted any woman since Mother walked out on us.''

Sebastian gave a hiss of denial, but they both knew it was true. Jamie had heard the story so often, from so many of the ranch hands and residents of Chalo Canyon, that it no longer had the power to sting.

Young, giddy Marianne Chavez had dealt her husband's pride a mortal blow when she'd run off with another man, leaving behind only a few scribbled lines and her five-month-old infant. Since that day, the old man had focused all his devotion, all his ambition, all his burning intensity on his son.

''Whether I trust Sydney or not isn't the only issue at stake here,'' Sebastian said fiercely. ''What if this movie she wants to make garners national attention? She'll focus attention on the ruins. The historical preservationists will get involved. They'll stir up the Hopi, try to save the village, maybe block the refill of the reservoir. Where will that leave us? We use that water for irrigation. The people in town depend on income from pleasure boaters and sportsmen.''

"I know, Dad, I know."

"Then why in God's name did you help her by flying her equipment into the canyon yesterday?"

Jamie had his own reasons for choppering into the canyon, but not ones he intended to share with the old man.

"Because your ploy to sabotage her shoot by scaring off the men she'd hired didn't work. I heard that Henry Three Pines intended to press his grandsons into service. I figured the sooner she got her gear and finished her shoot, the sooner she'd leave. That's what you really want, isn't it? For her to leave?"

"I..."

Sebastian hesitated, his black eyes strangely blank for a moment. Only then did Jamie notice the faint blue tinge to his father's lips. His heart jumped. For all their differences, for all he longed to throw off the burden of the old man's constant attention at times, he couldn't imagine a world without his father. Lunging around the edge of the trestle table, he grasped his father's arm.

"Dad? Are you okay?"

Sebastian gave a little shake, as if to throw off his momentary blankness, and lifted a hand to cover Jamie's. The strength of the older man's grip calmed the younger's galloping fears.

"I'm fine. Just worried about the harm this woman can cause you and Arlene. Your wife loves you, Son, with all her heart. That's a gift more precious than gold."

The suffocating feeling returned. Sooner or later, Jamie thought grimly, he was going to drown in all this love.

"I know."

Clawlike, the old man's fingers dug into his. "Promise me you won't go into the canyon again."

Strain put harsh lines in his aristocratic face. Sebastian looked old and tired...and almost frightened.

"I promise," Jamie said quietly.

"Good. Now go find your wife. I'm in the mood for a stiff bourbon and some charming company before dinner."

His heart swelling with pride, Sebastian watched his offspring stride to the door. James Sebastian Chavez was a good man, a son to be proud of. Sebastian had worked diligently over the years to stamp out every trace of his mother. She still surfaced in Jamie's rare flashes of temper or occasional urge to kick over the traces, but not as much of late. The boy had finally started to settle down, taken over more of the ranch and timber-harvesting operations.

Then Sydney Scott had returned to remind Jamie of his youth...and Sebastian of his past.

Gripping the back of his chair, he fought the memories that rose in his mind. Of his laughing young wife. Of his early struggles to provide her the luxuries she craved. Of his joy and her profound disgust when she learned she was pregnant. Of that last ride into Chalo Canyon when she'd been petulant and arguing and Sebastian had been cajoling, begging her as much as his stubborn pride would allow, to reconsider her decision to leave him.

No! He squeezed his eyes shut. He wouldn't remember that time, or the dark, bleak days that followed. She'd given him a son. If nothing else, Marianne had at least given him a son.

In his heart of hearts, Sebastian prayed constantly that Arlene would give Jamie a child. Unlike Marianne, Arlene wanted children. Even more, she wanted to please her husband. She loved him so desperately, starved herself to stay thin, spent exorbitant amounts each time she drove to Scottsdale to shop or have her hair done.

He would talk to Arlene, Sebastian decided. Maybe suggest she see a doctor. It was time, past time, she conceived. The problem, if there was one, had to be on her side, since Sebastian quietly paid a substantial allowance every month to the child Jamie had fathered even before he'd dallied with Sydney Scott.

Damn the woman, he thought again, remembering that near disaster of ten years ago. Damn her for opening the Pandora's box of the past.

Damn the woman!

Arlene dragged a brush through her feathery auburn hair, preparing to join her husband and father-in-law for dinner. With every stroke of the bristles, her thoughts kept returning to Sydney Scott. Damn her for tantalizing Jamie with visions of a world different from Chalo Canyon...and of a woman far different from his wife.

Dropping the brush, she stared into the gilded trifold mirror she'd imported from Italy with Sebastian's blessing. Her father-in-law had encouraged her to redecorate, urged her and Jamie to make the addition to the thick-walled adobe ranch house their home.

Now she knew that Jamie considered the luxurious wing a prison.

Her heart aching, Arlene examined her sculpted chin and pronounced cheekbones from three different angles. She didn't see the hollowed indentations or skin stretched skeletal tight, only the tiny pads in her upper lids. With a trembling finger, she stroked a little fatty fold. Despite her best efforts, it hadn't disappeared with fasting or facial exercise. She'd have to see a plastic surgeon in Phoenix or Scottsdale. She'd call tomorrow and make an appointment for next week. No, she'd wait until Sydney Scott left Chalo Canyon.

Damn the woman!

Ten miles away Reece unknowingly echoed the sentiments of Sebastian and his daughter-in-law. Like a persistent itch that couldn't be reached to scratch, Sydney irritated his thoughts.

Why couldn't he get the woman out of his mind?

He propped a boot on the low parapet that followed the crest of his dam. He'd come up to get some air, take a break before he and his team finished the revised cost estimates he'd promised his boss. Yet his wayward thoughts insisted on drifting to the crew at the ruins. Or more specifically, to the woman who directed them.

He ought to be calculating cubic yards of concrete, additional man-hours, the added economic impact to the surrounding area if the repairs took longer than originally anticipated. He let his gaze roam the now-empty chasm behind the massive concrete dam. At this point Reece couldn't say with any certainty when the reservoir would fill again. After two exhaustive days of e-mails, conference calls and sometimes heated discussions, his boss had decided to crunch the data and construct yet another 3-D finite element model. Since the modified repair program Reece was recommending would run some five million dollars more than originally budgeted for, he could understand Mike's reluctance to rush into it. At this rate, though, the actual repair work would take three years instead of three weeks.

Tomorrow he'd have to meet with a coalition of agricultural, environmental, recreational, Native American and business leaders to explain the added delay before a final decision.

Tonight…

Tonight. He kept wondering how the shoot was going, whether Sydney and her crew had any problems with the pulleys he'd rigged, whether he'd bump into her at the Lone Eagle Café later.

He hadn't seen her since yesterday, had only spoken to her briefly this morning when she'd called for clearance. Yet he couldn't shake the lingering image of her dancing green eyes when he'd tried to explain the rudimentary laws of physics, or his nagging regret that he'd turned down her offer of dinner last night. The more he thought about it, the more regret spiraled into lust. Hard on the heels of that lust came a twist of self-disgust when he remembered his spike of raw jealousy as he'd spotted Jamie Chavez oozing charm all over Sydney yesterday morning.

His boot hit the concrete.

What *was* it with this woman? How had she managed to get under his skin like this, as irritating as a cactus-pear rash and twice as annoying?

With a last glance up canyon, he headed back for the administration building and another bout with Westergaard's added-mass formula for computing incompressible and compressible fluid elements. That, at least, he could comprehend.

Happily unaware that she was the object of so much intense conjecture and irritation, Sydney loaded her crew and her equipment just as dusk dropped a veil of darkness over the canyon depths.

She hummed contentedly for most of the circuitous drive back to town. They'd had a good day, six full hours of sunlight. Even then, they'd needed artificial lighting for the interior shots. Trailing long, snaking cables, she and Zack and Katie had positioned the lights while a stooped-over Tish clambered through low doorways to pan interiors, even climbing down into a circular stone pit that had once served as a ceremonial kiva. Henry had provided some excellent narration on the secret rites held in the pit, accessible only from a small hole in the roof. She couldn't wait to get back to the motel to review the day's footage and listen to the tapes.

Her only disappointment was that the wind hadn't cooperated. It had gusted for a half hour or so this afternoon, then died without producing the eerie wail she wanted so much to catch on tape. Oh, well, what they had so far with the emergence sequence and the rainbow and today's shoot was good. Darn good!

Once at the motel, Albert pleaded weariness and went back to his room. Zack and Katie disappeared in the Blazer, heading for the nearest McDonald's, thirty-seven miles away.

Sydney and Tish settled in to go over the day's rushes. Changing into comfortable shorts and T-shirts, they left the door propped open to catch the night breeze and sat cross-legged on the floor of Sydney's room. Together they ran through the day's take, playing and replaying the tapes, recording information about the footage, making special note of those frames that caught the best contrast of light and shadow. Sydney would later transfer the information in her log onto her laptop computer. The computerized version made for easy reference when she began editing the raw material into a visual statement.

This was one of the most critical phases of a shoot. Each night she had to step out of her role as concept designer and director and look at what she'd actually shot, as opposed to what she'd intended to shoot. The two were often quite different. If she didn't capture the mood, the feeling she'd been seeking, she'd have to reshoot or alter her approach or perhaps rethink the statement she wanted to make.

"There! Hold it there!" She leaned closer to the video cassette player to copy a stop number. "I want to freeze that shot of the tower and use it as backdrop when we begin the tale of the Weeping Woman."

"Who's doing the narration?" Tish inquired as she jotted the stop number in her own log.

"I've got an actor lined up to read the script when we get back to L.A., but..."

"But what?"

Sydney tapped her pencil against her knee. "But I'm trying to think of a way to talk Reece Henderson into reading the script for me. He's got just the voice I want, all smooth rawhide and rough velvet."

The camera operator snorted. "If I wasn't married to a man who never lets me forget what a good thing I've got, I'd surely to goodness be trying to get Reece Henderson to do more than read to me."

"He's not interested in anything more."

"How do you know?"

"I offered to buy him dinner," Sydney admitted with a wry grin. "He turned me down flat."

"Turned you down? Uh-oh. That means he's either A, engaged...B, married...C, gay...or D, in love with his grandmother."

"According to him, it's not A or B, and from the kiss he laid on me the other night, I'm pretty sure it's not C. I can't speak to D, though."

"For the record," the rawhide and velvet voice drawled from the door, "it's E...none of the above."

Tish's head whipped around. Sydney merely groaned and closed her eyes.

"Tell me it's not him," she begged the other woman.

"Sorry, Syd, no can do." The camera operator's rich contralto vibrated with laughter. "Hello, Reece. Care to come in and join the discussion?"

"Not particularly. I just stopped by to tell your boss that you're clear to shoot tomorrow."

Tish elbowed her in the ribs. "Hear that, Syd?"

"Yes." She unscrewed her eyes enough to shoot her friend a glare before untangling her legs to push up from the green shag carpet.

"And to take her up on her offer," Reece added casually. "If it still stands?"

Sydney almost hit the shag again. Mortified by her clumsiness, she finally managed to get to her feet. The sight of Reece in the doorway, his black hair ruffled by the wind and those blue eyes glinting with amusement didn't exactly help restore her composure.

"Uh, yeah, I guess so."

Oh, that was brilliant! Telling herself to get a grip, she plastered on a wide smile.

"Yes, of course the offer still stands. When did you want to do it? Have dinner," she added immediately, but not fast enough to head off Tish's snicker.

Those awesome shoulders lifted in a shrug. "Have you already eaten?"

Sydney looked at him blankly. If asked, she could have recited the exact sequence of today's shoot, tossed off the precise amount of video and sound tape recorded to date, and even estimated the cost per minute of what they'd done so far to within a few dollars. But mundane matters like food took a moment to recall.

"No, she hasn't," Tish supplied, unfolding her long legs to rise gracefully to her feet. "She put me to work as soon as we got back to the motel. Now that I think about it, she skipped lunch, too."

"You haven't had dinner yet, either," Sydney pointed out to her too-helpful friend, still thrown off balance by Reece's unexpected appearance but recovering fast. "Why don't we all go?"

"No, thanks. I'm not used to climbing up and down cliffs without llamas nipping at my tush to keep me moving. I'm going to take a long, slow soak, then go over a few more of these reels."

Scooping up three of the minicassettes, she brushed by Reece with a wave of her red-tipped fingernails.

"Llamas?" he inquired.

"It's a long story." Locking her door behind her, Sydney slipped the key into her shorts pocket. "Where would you like to dine, the Lone Eagle Café or the Gas n' Git? Zack tells me the gas station has a tolerable selection of day-old doughnuts and hot dogs smothered in onions and Hormel chili."

"You choose. I'm easy."

Easy wasn't the adjective Sydney would have picked to describe Reece Henderson. Hard-assed had come to mind after their curt exchange of faxes a few weeks ago. Hard-edged was how she'd thought of him after he'd rescued her from her piñon tree. And yesterday he'd gone all professorial on her when he delivered his little lecture on fulcrums and trading distance for force or whatever.

Then there was that other aspect of his personality, the one that had prompted him to step into an awkward situation a few nights ago to spare Arlene any more embarrassment. And the curious quirk of character that had resulted in a mind-shattering kiss.

Sydney certainly wouldn't mind exploring that particular side of his personality just a bit more. She didn't want to do it at the Lone Eagle Café, though, with Lula Jenkins and the rest of the café's patrons listening to every word. Her disastrous affair with Jamie Chavez had provided the town with enough fodder for gossip to last the previous decade. She didn't want to fuel another ten years' worth.

"Let's hit the Gas n' Git," she suggested, as much to test Reece's resolve as her own. "We'll get our dinner in a bag and have a picnic. I know a great place not too far out of town to watch the stars."

Watching stars wasn't exactly what was on Reece's mind when he turned the Jeep off the road some miles south of town. With the scent of chili and onions teasing his nostrils, he steered the vehicle along a rutted dirt track. Low hanging pines swished their branches against the Jeep's roof.

He still couldn't quite believe he'd given in to the crazy impulse to take her up on her offer of dinner. He wouldn't have even stopped at her room on his way to the café, much less skulked outside her door like a hopeful peeping Tom, if he hadn't heard his name mentioned.

Hell, he wouldn't have stopped even then if he hadn't caught a flash of Sydney's slim, shapely legs stretched out on the pea-green shag carpet...the same bare legs that now tantalized Reece's senses almost as much as the onions and chili.

He'd never considered himself a leg man. He certainly couldn't claim to be a connoisseur like his older brother, Evan. Seeing Sydney in something other than her baggy fatigue pants gave him a new appreciation of Evan's particular fancy, however.

"It's not much farther," she said, breaking into

his silent contemplation of her shapely limbs. "Less than a mile. I think."

"You think?"

"It's been a while since I've been out here," she murmured absently. "Ten years, at least."

Which begged the question, Reece thought sardonically, of who she'd watched the stars with the last time. Was she taking him to one of her old trysting places?

The idea that Sydney had driven out to this isolated spot with Jamie Chavez and had ended up rolling around in the back seat shaved the edge right off Reece's concentration. The left front tire dropped into a rut, jouncing him and Sydney and their dinner.

She didn't comment on his driving skills, or lack thereof. With one hand braced against the dash and the other wrapped around the cardboard carryout box containing their dinner, she strained forward. Anticipation shimmered through the body detailed so precisely by that thin T-shirt tucked into thigh-riding shorts.

"Listen! There it is!" She swiveled, her face alive with eagerness in the scant moonlight filtering through the pines. "Can you hear it?"

Straining, Reece picked up a faint roar. "If you mean the river, I can."

"Not the river. The waterfall."

As soon as the Jeep cleared the trees and rolled to a stop a prudent distance from the river's edge, Sydney sprang out. Leaving Reece and the chili dogs behind, she scrambled up on a flat ledge. Hands shoved in the back pockets of her shorts, she drank in the vista of a tumbling, opalescent waterfall.

The falls weren't the most impressive Reece had ever seen. Having spent most of his adult life on the world's riverways, he'd viewed such spectacular spills as Canada's Churchill Falls and the spot on the border between Argentina and Brazil where the Iguacu River plunged almost three hundred feet over a two-mile-wide escarpment. This narrow fall couldn't be more than a twenty-five or thirty-foot drop, but the utter delight on Sydney's face told him she saw it with the eye of an artist, not a hydrologist.

He joined her on the ledge, almost as unsettled by the way her enchantment affected him as by his irritation of a few moments ago. The thought of her driving out here with Chavez still went down hard.

He might even have simply spent an hour downing cold chili dogs and taken her home if she hadn't turned to him at that moment, her eyes luminous in the moonlight.

"This was one of our special spots," she said softly. "Mine and my father's. Almost as special as the ruins. Since those were underwater most of the time, we'd come here when he wanted to fish or just talk."

"You came here with your dad?"

She nodded. "He was the fish and game warden at the state park while I was growing up. He…"

She swallowed, then tried a smile to hide the other emotions that flickered across her face.

"He died a few months ago."

Reece knew he was in trouble then. Big trouble. He forgot his earlier suspicions. Forgot that he didn't have time for any complications in his life now right.

The urge to comfort this woman gripped him and wouldn't let go.

He lifted a hand to stroke her cheek. He kept the touch gentle, soft. "I'm sorry."

Her smile got ragged at the edges. "Me, too. He was a good man. He loved the outdoors, and respected the natural order of things. You...you would have liked him."

As soon as she said it, Sydney knew the reverse was true as well. Her father would have liked Reece, would have admired his chosen profession. He'd often spoken of the utility of dams, of the way they harnessed nature's excesses so that man and river could peacefully coexist without the constant threat of floods or droughts.

But it wasn't the thought of her dad's approval that turned her head and brought her lips against Reece's palm. It was the warmth of his skin, the gentleness of his touch. That and the shivery delight that coursed through her at the contact.

He used his thumb to tip her head back, and the look in his eyes sharpened her delight into a spear of need so strong Sydney shook with it.

A frown feathered his brows. "Cold?"

"No. Yes." Another shiver rippled down her spine. "I don't know."

"The chili dogs might warm you up." His thumb traced her jawline, her lower lip. "Or I could."

"You choose," she whispered, echoing his earlier words to her. "I'm easy."

Chapter 8

As soon as she heard herself, Sydney winced.

Of all the stupid, idiotic, ill-chosen replies! She'd only been playing Reece's words back to him, mimicking his earlier suggestion that she choose their dinner locale, but in this particular situation the attribute "easy" carried a meaning she hadn't intended.

It also conjured up some instant, unpleasant memories. That was only one of the labels Sebastian had hung on her the awful night he'd found her in his son's arms. Chagrined that the memory could still sting, Sydney backpedaled, hard and fast.

"I know you've been filled in on every detail of my sordid past, but I didn't mean that as an invitation to anything more than a kiss."

"I didn't take it as anything more."

His thumb was at it again, soothing, stroking, distracting. She saw herself reflected in his eyes before they filled with a disturbing gleam.

"Maybe I can change your mind."

"You think?"

"A guy can only try," he murmured.

Sydney stood unmoving under the kiss, determined not to repeat her mistake of ten years ago. She'd tumbled into love…or thought she had…with a charming rogue, and let him distract her the last time she'd tried to film the ruins. She refused to let that happen again.

Maybe she should have thought of that before she'd invited Reece for a moonlit picnic at the falls. And maybe she'd wanted him to kiss her again, his mouth warm and hard on hers, his lips wickedly wonderful. But that insidious want did *not* mean she was going to fall into his bed when they returned to the motel, or invite him into hers.

She knew she had to make that clear when he lifted his head, his eyes at once questioning and rueful at her lack of response.

"I haven't changed my mind," she said quietly.

"Okay." His thumb made one more pass over her bottom lip before he dropped his hand. "Let's eat."

Surprised at his easy capitulation, Sydney watched him make his way back to the Jeep to retrieve their dinner. She hadn't expected him to give in that readily, and couldn't quite suppress an irrational pique that he had.

Telling herself to stop acting like a total jerk, she folded her legs under her Indian-style, sank down onto the rock shelf and waited for him to join her.

Reece kept his demeanor nonchalant as he returned with the soggy brown bag. Beneath that casual expression, however, frustration ate at him like fire ants at a picnic. It had taken everything he had and then some to walk away from Sydney a few moments ago. His body still ached with wanting her.

She didn't want him, though. She'd made that clear enough. Obviously he'd misread her signals, inferred more from her suggestion to drive out and watch the stars than she'd intended. Even worse, he'd let himself dwell far too much on that kiss the other night. She'd been playing to an audience then, he reminded himself with a twist of his lips. They both had.

Unfortunately, the reminder did nothing to relieve the ache in his lower body. As a result he made no objection when she swiped the last of the chili from a corner of her mouth, tossed her paper napkin and the empty beer cans into the cardboard carrier, and suggested they head back to the motel.

The conversation on the return trip flowed a good deal less freely than it had during the drive out. Reece didn't try to force it. Between the spicy chili and his irritatingly persistent desire for Sydney, both of which seemed to have settled like a lump in his gut, he had plenty to think about. Her annoyed exclamation when they turned into the motel parking lot gave him something altogether different to focus on.

"For Pete's sake!"

Reece slanted her a quick look. "What?"

"One of the crew must have been in my room. They left the door ajar."

Sure enough, a slice of light spilled from Unit Six.

Frowning, Reece pulled into the empty space in front of the open door.

"Who on your crew has a key to your room?"

"Everyone. We use it as sort of an on-site studio. We keep the master logs and the video cassette players in there."

Along with a lot of other expensive equipment, Sydney thought with a slash of worry. Extra strobes. Lenses in fitted cases. Spare batteries and digital sound units. She always upped her theft insurance when she went on-site, but a possible delay in the shooting schedule due to stolen equipment bothered her more than the idea that someone might have broken into her room. She was halfway to the door when Reece caught her arm.

"Stay here," he ordered quietly. "Let me check it out first."

Sydney considered herself a feminist and thoroughly competent in any number of ways, but respected the inarguable differences between the sexes. She had no problem at all with letting a tough, well-muscled male nudge her bedroom door open, flip on the lights and do a quick check before she ventured inside.

"You'd better get in here," he called.

Her heart pounding, she stepped through the door. She barely got a foot over the threshold before she froze. Shock constricted her veins, made each beat of her heart an agony. A low, animal cry rose in her throat.

"No!"

Cassettes littered the bed and the floor. Empty cassettes. Someone had ripped their guts out. Yard after yard of shiny brown tape formed a tangled mound in the middle of the green shag carpet.

Shattered, Sydney dropped down on her knees beside the mound. Her trembling fingers reached out, caught the end of a piece of videotape. It came free of the pile, less than a foot in length. Swallowing, she dug her hand into the tangled mass and grabbed a fistful. Loose ends fluttered like ribbons.

Three days work…destroyed. She'd lost the all important, once-in-a-decade emergence sequence. The rainbow footage. The first view of the glistening ruins. The interiors.

She wanted cry. She would have…if she hadn't used up a lifetime supply of tears during the months of Pop's illness. Now she could only close her fist over those tattered bits of videotape and squeeze until the knuckles showed white.

"Sydney, I'm sorry."

Reece came down on one knee beside her. Concern darkened his eyes. Anger etched deep grooves on either side of his mouth.

"Did you make any backups?"

It took a moment before she could speak. Her throat worked, forcing out the words.

"Of course. But they're working copies, not good enough to print from."

"I see." He eyed the tangled mess in her hand. "Any chance you can splice it together?"

"The person who did this made sure he didn't leave enough for me to salvage."

"He?"

"Sebastian," she hissed, fury slicing through her dismay.

Wave after wave of hot anger spilled into her. Scalding, raging, a conflagration that consumed her. Her hand shook so badly the ends of the tape danced.

"Sebastian told me I wasn't welcome here, that he wanted me gone, but I never thought he'd stoop to something this...this vicious!"

"We don't know for sure he did it."

"I know," she said savagely.

She looked so wild, so fierce...so damned *hurt*...that the need to comfort her grabbed Reece right by the throat again.

Before he could give in to that need, she surged to her feet. The air around her almost vibrated with the force of her anger.

"I'll check with the others on my crew. Maybe they saw something."

"Good idea," Reece said, reaching for the phone. "While you do that, I'll call the sheriff."

The group that gathered outside Sydney's room over the next half hour included not only her crew and Deputy Sheriff Joe Martinez, but Martha Jenkins, proprietor of the Lone Eagle Motel, her sister, Lula, and several of Reece's engineers and construction workers, drawn by the noise and the flashing strobe lights.

No one, it turned out, had seen or heard anything. But Tish, to her boss's profound relief, reminded Sydney that she'd taken a handful of cassettes to her room. She had the all-important emergence sequence reels and a few of the exterior shots in her possession.

Sydney pounced on them like a hen would a missing chick. "Thank God!"

Clutching the cassettes to her chest, she thought furiously. She could reshoot everything else except the rainbow...*if* Reece gave her unlimited access to the ruins and *if* the rains held off and *if* she worked herself and her crew dawn to dusk for the next six days straight.

She'd have to fly back to Chalo Canyon after the reservoir refilled to shoot the exteriors across the water. If that didn't fit with Tish's schedule, she could shoot that footage herself. That would push her deadline for finishing the first cut up several weeks, and not give her as much time as she'd wanted for the fine cut, but she might still make her October viewing with PBS.

Her eyes narrowed with grim determination. She could do it! She had to do it!

She'd invested all her personal resources, everything she had left after her father's hospital and funeral bills in this project and in her new studio. If pressed, she could give up the studio and try to recoup some of the outlay for all that expensive equipment, but she'd staked more than money on this documentary. She'd made a promise to her father and put her professional reputation on the line with her backers. She wouldn't allow anyone to stop her. Anyone!

She swept the small crowd, saw Reece talking to the deputy sheriff. The same man had taken her statement about the Blazer she'd sent to the bottom of the gorge. His brows had climbed when he'd unfolded his rangy frame from the sheriff's vehicle and seen who waited for him.

Sydney had told him what she could about to-night's incident, but the deputy had aimed more questions at Reece than at her. Probably because Reece had checked the door and windows for signs of forced entry. He was the one who found the jimmied lock on the bathroom window, prevented the others from entering her room and generally kept his cool while Sydney had come so close to losing hers.

Reece had understood her fury, though. Those moments inside the room when they'd knelt knee-to-knee on the floor, she'd heard the sympathy in his voice, seen the outrage on his face. If she was another kind of woman, if this was a different time or place, she could easily have leaned into him, howled out her anger and frustration, drawn from his strength. She'd hidden her feelings for so long, though. Been strong for herself and for her father.

Now…

Now more than ever she had to stick to the decision she'd made back there at the falls. She couldn't let Reece distract her, couldn't give in to this crazy urge to lock the door on the shambles in her room and lose herself and her worries in his arms for a few hours.

"Guess I have all I need here," the deputy said a few moments later, flipping his notebook shut. "I dusted the bathroom window and cassettes for prints. We'll match them against the samples you and your crew gave us, Ms. Scott. In the meantime, you might want to move your things into another room. Martha, you got one available?"

The motel proprietress huffed. "Until that reservoir fills up again, Joe, we've got more empties than I want to think about. I'll go get a key."

"We never had a break-in before," her sister added, her black eyes lively. "You sure do generate your share of excitement round these parts, girl."

The dry observation was accompanied with such a sympathetic hug that the perpetrator of all this excitement could only smile.

"Not by choice, Lula."

She edged past the café owner to speak privately to the deputy. "When do you plan to interview Sebastian Chavez?"

Martinez knuckled his straw sheriff's hat to the back of his head, clearly not looking forward to the prospect of asking the county's most powerful landowner to account for his whereabouts tonight.

"I'll drive out to the Chavez place first thing in the morning."

"Let me know what he has to say."

"Yes, ma'am. In the meantime, I need you to come up with an estimated value of the destroyed property."

Frustration added its bite to Sydney's still-simmering anger. In dollars and cents, the actual value wouldn't run to more than the cost of a dozen replacement cassettes. In lost time and footage, the figure could easily reach five figures.

"I will."

He pulled his hat down onto his forehead, tipped it politely. "Ms. Scott. Reece."

"Get your logs," she told her crew as the squad car pulled out of the parking lot. "We'll do a damage assessment and work out a new shoot schedule as soon as I get the key to another room.''

Reece opted to wait beside Sydney until Martha returned.

"You okay?" he asked quietly while the others dispersed.

"Yes." She blew out a breath, still raw, still tense, but no longer shaking with fury. "I'll have to hustle to make up the lost footage."

He got the message. She was going to be busy from here on out. Even more to the point, she wanted unlimited access to the area behind the dam. Unfortunately Reece couldn't grant it.

"I should have a decision on my recommended repairs to the dam by tomorrow," he told her, hoping it was true. "I'll let you know as soon as I can how long you've got to shoot. In the meantime, press ahead."

"Thanks."

Her eyes were solemn, bereft of the dancing light that made them sparkle like sunlight refracted through green quartz. He hated leaving her like this. Hated the idea that someone had gained such easy access to her room. Wondered how the hell her safety had become his personal responsibility since the morning he'd pulled her from that piñon tree.

The memory of her near tragedy curled his hands into fists…and sent a sudden, icy chill into his chest. He went still, thinking back, seeing in his mind once more the hairpin turn, the rain-softened shoulder, the slab of sandstone that had tumbled into the road.

He needed to go back, check that site again before

he voiced any suspicions or raised more doubts. In the meantime…

Martha's bustling return broke into his racing thoughts. Reece had time for only a final touch, a brief caution. His hand came up, tucked a wayward strand of mink-colored hair behind her ear. His knuckles brushed her cheek.

"Be careful out there."

"I will."

He waited while the two women inspected Units Twelve and Fourteen.

Sydney opted for Twelve, then bade him goodnight. To her continuing consternation, his touch lingered on her skin long after she'd moved her things into her new room.

Dawn hadn't yet broken when Sydney stood at the bathroom sink the next morning, already outfitted in her working uniform of high-topped canvas boots, fatigue pants and a ruby-red stretch top layered with a sweater that would tie loosely around her hips when the sun rose. She'd drawn her hair back, pulling the tail through the back of her ballcap to keep it out of her face. All she needed was moisturizer to protect her skin and she was ready to start over.

She slathered it on, her busy fingers slowing when they reached the spot on her cheek Reece had touched last night. For a big man, his touch was surprisingly gentle.

Regret flowed, sharp and stinging, before she shrugged it aside. She had work to do!

One by one her crew dragged out of their rooms and began ferrying equipment to the van and the

Blazer. They had the vehicles almost loaded when Henry Three Pines drove up in his rusted pickup. Sydney didn't really need the services of a guide any longer. By now, she knew every rock and twist in the path leading into the canyon. When she'd hinted as much to Henry yesterday, however, he merely smiled and said he wished to honor his old friend's memory by aiding his daughter in her quest.

This morning it appeared he wished to do more than honor a memory or merely act as guide. Reaching into the truck, he lifted out a rifle and tucked it in the crook of his arm.

A sleepy-eyed Zack came awake fast, dancing back a step when he spotted the weapon. "Whoa, dude! Is that thing, like, loaded?"

"Why would I carry it if it wasn't?"

"You, er, haven't forgotten how to handle it, have you?"

Henry's seamed face folded into a smile at the folly of youth. "Some things a boy must learn and a man never forgets."

"If you say so," Zack conceded doubtfully, edging around the barrel to dump his load in the van.

Sydney, too, made a cautious circuit of the gleaming gun barrel. She hadn't yet succumbed to the stereotypical L.A. resident's predilection for powerful cars and even more powerful personal handguns.

"What is this?" she asked Henry. "Why are you armed?"

"Reece called me last night and told me what happened. He and I agreed we must remain wary until the one who destroyed your film is caught."

She didn't bother to point out that she was using

videotape, not film. Such distinctions meant nothing to people outside the industry.

"Remaining wary is one thing, having you ride shotgun is another. I'm not sure about this, Henry."

"You look to your film," he replied with unruffled calm. "Reece and I will look to you."

Sydney wasn't sure she wanted to be "looked to," even by this longtime friend. The placid expression in Henry's black eyes told her it was a waste of time to argue, however, and time was her most precious commodity right now. The eastern sky already showed the first purple streaks of dawn. She wanted to be in place at the ruins to catch the full sun when it broke over the eastern rim.

She'd talk to Reece later, she decided, make sure he understood that she wanted in on any further decisions regarding her or her crew. Right now, though, she had to get her team ready to roll.

Long fingers of sunlight and shadow slanted across the canyon rim when Reece pulled up at the switchback turn where Sydney's vehicle had parted company with the road. His men had removed the slab of tumbled limestone blocking the road and added a temporary metal guardrail to keep vehicles a safe distance from the shoulder. The road was passable again, but it wasn't the makeshift repairs that interested Reece.

His eyes grim and intent, he climbed the striated cliff that edged the road. It took a few moments to find the scar left when the smaller projection had broken free. As yet unweathered by wind or rain, the slash showed pale white against the salmon color of the cliffs.

Reece fingered the scar, followed it up one side, down the other. He wasn't sure what he was looking for, but he sure as hell knew when he found it.

His jaw tightening, he traced the small gouges. They could have been made by a falling rock hitting against the surface. Or by a chisel or crowbar positioned at precisely the right angle to pry loose a slab of stone and send it tumbling to the road below.

He studied them for long moments before climbing down to the road. Back at the Jeep, he pulled out his cell phone, put in a call to the county offices and settled down to wait for Joe Martinez.

The deputy took almost an hour to arrive at the scene. In the interim, Reece received two calls from his on-site engineer and placed one to his boss. The Bureau of Reclamation's supercomputer had kicked out the latest analysis using the revised data Reece had provided after his visual inspection of the exterior. The powers-that-be didn't feel they warranted a modification to the fix as currently designed and contracted for.

"We've spent most of the night going over the specifications and design," his boss said wearily when Reece got him on the phone. "The specifications that you helped draft, I might point out."

"Those were done using computer-generated models and X-ray scans made by underwater divers. My gut now tells me these stress fractures run deeper than we're seeing."

"The revised data you sent us doesn't support that

gut feel. We need to move on this project, Reece. The heavier-than-expected rainfall this summer has elevated water levels all along the Colorado River System. We've got to get this dam up and fully operational again before the next flood season.''

"You're not telling me anything I don't know here, Mike.''

His long-suffering supervisor vented some of his own frustration. "I'm taking all the flak I can handle on this project, Reece. Every day the dam is out of service is costing the government megabucks in lost power generation and water income. I can't justify additional delays without something more specific than your intestinal rumblings.''

It was an old dilemma, one Reece had struggled with since he'd joined the Bureau of Reclamation. Whenever a dam went down, disrupting power and water supply, pressure mounted hourly to get it back in service.

Still, safety was and always had been the first consideration. Reece had worked with Mike long enough to know he'd go toe-to-toe with the Bureau's commissioner, the secretary of the interior, even the president himself if he had the facts and figures to support him.

That Reece hadn't been able to supply those facts or figures churned like acid in his stomach.

"All right,'' he conceded reluctantly. "I'll notify the contractors to proceed. But I reserve the right to halt work if I find anything at the core that worries me.''

"Of course. We want this done, but we want it done right.''

Reece flipped the phone shut and tucked it in his shirt pocket. The need to get back to the dam pulled at him. He had to go over the blasting schedule a final time, make sure the subcontractors were ready to roll with the hundreds of cubic yards of cement needed for the repairs, brief the civic leaders in the area...including Sebastian Chavez.

The thought of Chavez kept Reece sitting right where he was. Was the old man behind the destruction of Sydney's videotapes? Had he made those chisel marks in the limestone? *Were* they chisel marks?

Chapter 9

"I don't know," Joe Martinez muttered when he finally arrived at the site of Sydney's near slide into oblivion. Squatting on his heels, he fingered the marks in the limestone. "Could be cuts. Could be gouges made by falling rocks."

"Can you test the surface of the stone for metal traces?"

Martinez pushed his hat forward to scratch the back of his head. "I'll have to check with our crime-scene technical unit, but I doubt they've got that kind of sophisticated equipment. We might be able to send samples to the State Forensics Lab. Depending on their workload, it could take weeks to get an answer."

Reece had expected that answer. "Maybe I can speed things up a little. I worked a mine-flooding problem with a metallurgist on the governor's Science and Advisory Board a few years ago. She has access to a scanning and transmission electron microscope that would pick up even microstructural traces of metal. Maybe I can talk her into taking a look at this rock.''

''Sounds good to me.''

''The piece that broke off...or was pried off...is still lying in the middle of the road. If you can get one of your men to haul it down to the Arizona Geological Survey Center in Tucson, I'll call ahead to let Dr. Kingsley know it's on the way.''

''Consider it done.''

Martinez rose, dusting his hands on his pants. His boots clattered on stone as he inched his way back down to the road. Once on level land, his black eyes rested thoughtfully on Reece.

''Are you thinking the same person who slashed Ms. Scott's tapes last night might have tried to keep her from making them in the first place?''

''The possibility occurred to me. Did you talk to Sebastian Chavez this morning?''

''I talked to both him and his son. Mr. Chavez had dinner at home with his son and daughter-in-law last night, then put in some late hours in his office.''

''Anyone see him during those hours?''

''Jamie didn't. He was out in one of the barns with a sick horse most of the night. Mrs. Chavez... Arlene...said she saw the lights on in Sebastian's office when she went up to bed.''

''So none of them really has an alibi.''

''As yet,'' Martinez pointed out, ''none of them needs one. We matched the prints I lifted from the bathroom window to Martha Jenkins, and those on the videocassettes to Ms. Scott and her camera operator. We have no witnesses and no evidence that one of the Chavez family perpetrated the vandalism."

"Just Sydney's gut feel," Reece muttered, unamused by the irony.

Martinez hitched up his holster and slid into the driver's seat of his dust-streaked vehicle. "I'll see that rock gets to Tucson this afternoon. In the meantime, you might advise Ms. Scott to keep her eyes open."

"I already have."

Reece would do more than just offer advice. Between them, he and Henry Three Pines would do their damnedest to make sure she didn't meet with any more unexpected accidents. He'd talked to the Hopi headman at some length last night, learned more about what happened ten years ago. That debacle had cost Sydney her pride and her father his job. Reece intended to see that it didn't now cost her her life.

His overdeveloped sense of responsibility had kicked in again, big-time. His brothers would have recognized the signs immediately. The slashing frown. The white-knuckled grip on the steering wheel when he climbed into the Jeep. The square angle of his jaw. Only Reece knew that responsibility had gotten all mixed up with something that went deeper than mere attraction, zinged right past lust, and smacked up against want. Or need. Or whatever the hell it was that twisted around inside him whenever he thought about Sydney.

Putting the Jeep into reverse, he made a cautious

three-point turn and headed back along the rim road. The deep gorge, empty of the waters that had filled it for the past ten years, stretched for miles on his right. Red cliffs crowded the road on the left. Reece kept a careful eye on the twists and turns, but his mind stayed fixed on Sydney and those gouges in the stone.

He'd talk to her tonight at the motel, he decided. Tell her about the marks, about his talk with Henry and Joe Martinez. His stomach tightened at the thought of the hurt and fear that might come with this latest threat.

As if Reece needed anything else to add to the tension building in him more with each passing hour, storm clouds started piling up just after two that afternoon.

He didn't see them until he walked out of the administration building with the prime contractor, who planned to start blasting tomorrow. The moment they stepped outside, the wind whipped at the rolled schematic in the contractor's hand.

"The front's coming in from the north," he observed, eyeing the bank of black clouds. "Hope it blows through without dumping too much rain in the mountains, or we'll have to work around a gully-washer tomorrow."

"I hope so, too," Reece muttered.

Automatically he leaned over the parapet to check the floodgates. Newer dams were constructed with floating, roller-type caissons that moved up and down to control the water flow. On older structures like

this one, the gates were simple up-and-down mech-
anisms.

They now stood fully open, as they had since the
reservoir began draining. Reece's men could drop
them quickly if necessary to control flooding, but that
would cause a buildup behind the dam and subse-
quently drown all the equipment the contractor had
positioned at the base of the structure in anticipation
of beginning repairs.

It could also flood the area behind the dam...up
to and including the Anasazi ruins.

Damn!

He considered pulling Sydney and her crew out of
the area. He even dug his mobile phone out of his
pocket. Only the knowledge of how desperately she
needed to remake the destroyed footage kept him
from punching in her number.

He would watch the weather reports, he decided
grimly. Check the computer every half hour for up-
dates from the various monitoring stations maintained by the Bureau on the water level upriver. That
way he could allow Sydney as much time as possible
at the ruins. He'd give her a heads-up, though, just
in case.

Her voice came over the airwaves, breathless, dis-
tracted, impatient. "Rain? What rain? I don't see any
clouds."

"They're piling up in the north. Stick your head
out of the cave and look."

He heard a thump, the sound of boots on rock, a
muffled curse. A moment or two later she came back
on, alive with excitement.

"The wind's picked up! Albert's recording just the sounds I want."

"Sydney, the clouds..."

"Listen!"

She must have stuck the phone out the face of the cave. A low whistling moan sounded through the receiver, lifting the hairs on the back of Reece's neck.

"Can you hear the wail?"

"I hear it. Sydney, the clouds. "

"Don't worry! I'll watch them. The last time I heard that wail, I took a short slide down a long cliff. I won't let anything distract me so much that I get washed down a river."

"I'll call you when and if I think you should leave."

"Thanks."

"Let me know if you depart the area before that."

"Will do."

She snapped her phone shut, obviously eager to get back to her project. Reece did the same.

To his relief, the rain held off upriver for an hour, then another. By the time he called it a day and sent his crew home just after six, however, the sky to the north had blackened ominously.

He still hadn't heard from Sydney. He didn't doubt she was taking advantage of every hour of light, every shrill whistle of wind. Tossing aside his hard hat, Reece climbed into the Jeep. He could call her, tell her to come in. Or he could make a quick trek down the canyon to check on her progress and suggest she drive back to town with him. That would give him the opportunity to tell her about the marks in the sandstone.

Or so he rationalized as he pulled up beside the Blazer fifteen minutes later. The absence of the van indicated Sydney had sent at least part of her crew back to town. With the black clouds whipping closer by the minute, Reece made his way down the cliffs to the riverbed.

When he reached the film crew's temporary base camp set up below the ruins, Reece discovered that everyone had departed except the earringed, earphoned Zack and Henry Three Pines.

"Is he listening to the wind?" Reece asked, indicating the kid.

Henry's wrinkled face creased even more. "No. I believe he listens to one called Marilyn Manson."

Absorbed in the grunge rocker's lyrics, Zack didn't hear Reece's approach. He jumped half a foot in the air when tapped on the shoulder. Ripping off the earphones, he spun around.

"Geez, dude, go easy on the heart muscles!"

"Sorry. Where's your boss?"

"Up in the ruins, retrieving the mikes. She sent me down to pack up the rest of the equipment before the rain hits."

"Better get with it."

A pierced eyebrow lifted, but Reece was too used to giving orders and Zack too used to following them to argue.

"I'll have to make two trips," he grumbled. "Albert was feeling punk and left half of his gear for me to haul back to the van."

"Load up what you can carry and head out with

Henry. I'll bring the rest and follow with Sydney when she finishes here.''

"Thanks, man!"

Sydney still hadn't appeared when Zack and Henry trudged off. Reece waited another fifteen minutes before he lost patience and called out to her. His shout bounced off the cliff wall a couple of times before the now-howling wind caught it and whipped it away.

Muttering, he headed for the aluminum ladder. She was probably lost in her creative visions again, or so determined to capture the wind's wail that she hadn't even noticed how dark the sky had grown.

Reece noticed it, though, *and* the lightning that snaked out of a cloud when he was still a few feet shy of the cave floor. Cursing, he scrambled up the last rungs and threw himself clear of the metal posts a mere second before another flash zigzagged across the sky. Picking himself up, he dusted off and watched as the supercharged ions lit the clouds from the inside out.

Well, hell!

No way either he or Sydney were going back down that ladder until the storm had passed.

Which is exactly what he informed her when she appeared a few seconds later, draped in black wire and assorted mikes.

"You're kidding!"

He shoved a hand through his hair, raking down the wind-whipped spikes. "A lightning bolt peaks at about twenty thousand amps. That's not something I'd kid about."

"Twenty thousand?" She threw the darkened sky

a wary, respectful look. "Guess we'll have to make ourselves comfortable and wait this one out."

Lifting the wires from around her neck, she started to settle in the shelter of a half-standing stone wall. Reece caught her elbow.

"We'd better go farther back into the ruins, away from the ladder."

More than happy to put as much stone as possible between her and the potential to end up as stir-fry, Sydney wove past crumbled wall and ducked under a low lintel, plunging instantly into inky blackness.

Reece followed more slowly, letting his eyes adjust to the gloomy interior as he picked his way over fallen chunks of shale.

"Back here!"

Her voice echoed through the ruins, luring him on. After the first few paces, the walls closed in. Ceilings dropped, crowding so low he whacked his head against lintels twice. The only light came from the occasional brilliant flashes that lit the narrow window slits. Even after three days in the sun, the village smelled dank from its long, underwater sleep.

"This room's relatively intact," Sydney announced when he bent almost double to enter a small chamber.

It was tucked away under the lowest portion of the overhang. A single narrow window looked out over the canyon. Reece stumbled and almost tripped in a smooth, oblong depression in the stone floor. The trough gave him a clue to the room's use. It was probably a kitchen or a storeroom, he guessed. A place where the Anasazi ground and stored their maize.

Wary of the low ceilings, he felt his way along the wall until he spotted the pale blur of Sydney's face.

"Didn't you bring a flashlight up here with you?" he asked.

"Several, but they're in my backpack, which at this moment is sitting a few feet from the ladder." She looked up at him hopefully. "I don't suppose you have anything to munch on with you?"

"Sorry." He dropped down beside her, his back to the wall. "Don't you ever eat regular meals?"

"I don't have time for them when I'm on location." She thought about that for a moment. "Or when I'm at home. Food isn't real high on my list of priorities."

"Except at moments like this, when you can't work," he guessed.

Her teeth gleamed white in the murky gloom. "Especially at moments like this. That's why I keep Zack on the payroll. He generally remembers to order in a pizza or go pick up Chinese."

"Just out of curiosity, what currency do you pay him in? Silver nose rings?"

"That, and one-on-one instruction in the art of documentary filmmaking. Don't let his appearance fool you. He's an honors grad of UCLA's cinematography school."

"He could use some work on his professional image," Reece returned, stretching out his legs.

"Couldn't we all? Take you, for instance. When I first saw you in your jeans and straw cowboy hat, I didn't connect you with an engineer."

"You mean the day you drove off the cliff? Your

appearance was a little misleading, too. Anyone seeing you then might have mistaken you for a ditzy,
artistic type.''

''I did *not* drive off that cliff. And as I recall, that's
exactly how you thought of me.''

It was the perfect lead-in to tell her that her accident might have been staged. Reece had set up the
intro with deliberate casualness. He hated to frighten
her or put that fierce, hurt look in her eyes again.
Not that he could see her eyes at this moment, but
he hadn't forgotten the anguish in her face last night.

He'd just opened his mouth to tell her about the
gouges in the stone when nature accomplished exactly what he was trying to avoid. In one thunderous
boom, it scared the bejebers out of the woman next
to him.

The sky split. Lightning cracked seemingly right
outside the window. The tiny chamber lit with brilliant white light, causing Sydney to scream like a
banshee and give a credible imitation of a badger
trying to burrow inside Reece's shirt.

He wrapped his arms around her, soothing, stroking, wincing when her elbow augered into his hip-
bone. After a long, booming roll of thunder, he gave
her the all clear.

''It's okay. Sydney, it's okay.''

''That's what you say now!'' she muttered into his
shirt pocket. ''A moment ago you were talking
twenty million amps!''

''Twenty thousand.''

''Whatever.''

He might have convinced her to dig herself out of
his shirt if the rain he'd anticipated all afternoon

hadn't broken loose at that moment. It came down in sheets, driven by the howling wind, and blew sideways through the slitted window.

With the tested reflexes of a man who'd grown up with four rough and ready brothers, Reece rolled away from the drenching spray, taking Sydney with him.

She ended up in his lap. For the life of him, Reece couldn't say whether that was intentional or not on his part. However she got there, she stayed right where she was, her shoulder pressed his chest, her hair damp and silky under his nose.

He'd tell her about the gouge marks on the stone later, he decided. Right now he'd simply share his warmth and hold her until she lost the shivers generated by fright or by the chill brought in by the rain and the darkness.

His good intentions lasted exactly as long as it took for Sydney to shift to a more comfortable position in his lap. Her body contacted his everywhere it shouldn't. Reece went from loose and relaxed to hard and tight in two and a half seconds flat.

She couldn't miss his sudden stiffening. She shifted again and caused a sort of chain reaction. Her head came up, cracking Reece on the underside of his chin. Her elbow did its thing on his hip again. Her breast pushed into his chest, and he got even harder.

Flattening her palms on his chest, she pushed upright. He couldn't see her expression clearly in the darkness, only hear her quick, uneven breath. He was trying to think of some way to pass off the awkward moment when her voice came to him, soft and edgy and just a little breathless.

"Reece?"

"Yes?"

"Last night, at the waterfall?"

A charged silence filled the chamber. Reece had to speak carefully around the jagged shards of heat slicing into his throat.

"What about last night at the waterfall?"

"I wanted you to kiss me. Almost as much as I want you to kiss me now."

He resisted the driving urge to do just that. "I hear a 'but' in there."

She took his face in her palms, her own a pale blur in the darkness. "But I want to be honest with you. Trust me when I tell you that you don't have to worry that I'll repeat my mistake of ten years ago. I won't tumble into love with you just because I…because we…" Her breath left on a long, determined sigh. "Because of this."

For reasons totally beyond Reece's comprehension, Sydney's earnest assurance that she wouldn't fall in love with him scratched his pride. He didn't *want* her to fall for him, for Pete's sake! Until this moment his only thought was to lock her body to his, to slide her under him and hear her gasp and pant and cry out in a fever of delight.

Now he wanted more, but with Sydney's soft, moist lips and eager hands destroying his concentration, not to mention his control, he was damned if he could decide what.

Later, he decided. He'd deal with this irrational response to her declaration later. Right now, the woman leaning into him, her mouth hungry on his, was all he could handle.

He tumbled back, taking care that she landed atop him, cushioning her from the hard rock. Tongues met. Knees tangled. Hands slid, shaped, cupped. The cave's darkness, split at intermittent moments by flashes of light, wrapped around them. Rain shot through the narrow window and sizzled on stone. Reece didn't notice the damp, didn't worry about the rain. Sydney filled his senses. Like a wild, powerful river rushing through giant turbines, she roared in his ears, churned his blood, set him on fire at every pulse point in his body.

She was all long legs and soft breasts, hungry mouth and sweet, tart tongue. Reece stroked and nipped and sucked the skin of her jaw, her throat, the curve of her neck. Each taste increased his hunger, each glide of his fingers on her hips and waist sparked small fires. He rolled her a little to one side, found the soft mound of breast flattened against his chest.

Stretched atop Reece, her legs tangled with his and her body fitted to his, Sydney marveled at the magic he created with every touch, every scrape of his teeth and tongue. She'd never burned like this. Never wanted so badly. The realization worried her enough to pull back for a moment, her breath almost as loud and harsh as the rain gusting through the window.

"Reece…"

"I know," he growled. "You don't want to repeat your mistake of ten years ago."

His hands tangled in her hair, holding her head

still. Even in the dim light, Sydney saw the blue fire in the eyes that blazed up at her.

"Just for the record, though, I'm not Jamie Chavez."

She sucked in a shocked breath. "I know that. I never thought... I didn't mean to imply—"

"And this isn't ten years ago."

He dragged her head down and kissed her with stunning intensity. His mouth ravaged hers as if to prove his point that he was nothing like her charming, feckless first love. She felt swamped, consumed, almost savaged, and something primitive in her stirred. In this cave, in this darkness, with lightning crashing outside and hard stone beneath, she had a fleeting sense of what the Anasazi women must have felt centuries ago when their men came back from the hunt to claim them.

For a moment the line between reality and fantasy blurred. The present merged into the past. A feeling of powerlessness invaded Sydney. Almost panic. Like the Weeping Woman of Chalo Canyon, she felt trapped, bound to this hard, muscular man with something stronger than rope, more binding than chains.

She could stop what was happening with a word, a single push on his shoulder. She knew that. Reece wouldn't follow this savage kiss with an equally savage possession if she dragged her head up and gasped out a protest.

She tried to do it. Even managed to lift her head an inch or two before the primal need stirring in her belly smothered the protest. Instincts deeper than thought, older than time, drove her. She wanted to feel him, run her hands over his arms and back and shoulders, taste his salty skin. Surrendering to that dark, primal need, she tugged at his shirt, dragging the tail free of his jeans so she could slide her hands under it. He made a sound that could have been hunger, could have been triumph. Before she could decide which, he'd stripped off her tank top.

The stretchy top ended up under her, wadded into a ball, cushioning her shoulders from the hard stone. His shirt followed a moment later, providing a pad for her hips. She'd barely registered the cool, damp air on her skin when Reece dipped his head for a hot, greedy exploration of her breasts. He took the peaks between his teeth, teasing, worrying, raising stinging needles that arched her back and had her panting.

She was slick with sweat and wet with need when his hand went to the zipper on her shorts. The brush of his knuckles on her belly hollowed her stomach. She wanted to mate with this man. Wanted to take him into her, feel him inside her, test her will and her femininity against his awesome strength. Yet even the primal instinct that drove her couldn't completely subdue her twentieth-century common sense.

"We can't," she panted, her voice raw with regret. "I want to. Believe me, I want to! But I'm not— I haven't— I don't have any protection," she ended on a wail.

Above her, his mouth curved in a slow, wicked grin. "Didn't I tell you about my brothers? I have four of them, one younger, three older."

This wasn't exactly the moment Sydney would have chosen to exchange family histories. She could barely breathe, much less pretend an interest in anything other than the fingers making small circles just above her bellybutton.

"From the time I was twelve," he murmured, watching the rapid rise and fall of her stomach with great interest, "Jake and Evan and Marsh made sure I left the house prepared for any eventuality."

She managed a shaky laugh. "Twelve, huh?"

"We Hendersons matured early," Reece explained, his grin deepening to a slash of white teeth and unabashed masculinity.

Early or late, they'd certainly matured. This one had, anyway. Sydney couldn't help noticing how much when he shed his jeans. He was, to put it simply, magnificent. Rippling skin stretched tightly over corded muscles and lean hips. A dusting of black hair created shadows on his chest and lower belly.

When he stretched out beside her, the instincts Sydney had fought to subdue just a moment before went out of control. She lifted her hips so he could slide off her shorts, taking her panties with them, and welcomed him eagerly when he covered her. His knees nudged hers apart, his mouth descended once more, hard, demanding.

When his hand slipped between her legs, desire burst into a blinding, white-hot flame. Within seconds the flame became a raging inferno. To Sydney's astonishment and complete mortification, she felt herself climaxing. She stiffened her legs. Tried to fight it. Couldn't stop the spiraling sensations.

"Reece!"

"It's all right." His mouth was hot on hers, his

hand so skilled that a groan ripped from the back of her throat. "Let it go."

"As...if...I...have...any—" Her head went back. Her body arched. "Oh! Ooooh!"

Her last coherent thought was that Reece had chosen the right profession after all. He certainly knew his way around dams. With one wicked twist of his fingers, he opened all the floodgates. Pleasure roared through and over and around Sydney, until she was sure she'd drown in it.

She was still gasping for air when he thrust into her. Skillfully, sinfully, he filled the reservoir once more, bringing her to another shattering release before following her over the crest.

Chapter 10

Sydney didn't notice that the storm had passed until she stretched, replete and catlike in her languorous contentment. The lazy twist brought her head around and the window into view. She stared at the narrow slit for long moments before recognizing the whitish glow outside as moonlight.

The pale wash of gold stirred her. She'd love to capture the ruins in this light. Reece had told her that he'd sent Zack and Henry back to town with most of the equipment. Maybe they'd left a minicam behind. Not one of Tish's expensive Cannons. She'd have taken those with her. But Sydney's personal camera, snug and safe in its waterproof case, might still be there.

Yet, as much as the moonlight tugged at her, she couldn't bring herself to move. She didn't want to untangle her arms and legs, or relinquish the damp heat of Reece's powerful body pressed so intimately on hers.

Even more to the point, she wasn't ready to examine the nagging little worry that crept into her head. Maybe, just maybe she hadn't learned her lesson of ten years ago as thoroughly as she thought she had.

She could love this man, she thought with a catch in her throat. Easily. After their explosive joining, Sydney knew instinctively that she could make love with Reece Henderson again and again and never lose the wonder of it, the sheer, carnal delight.

The thought scared the heck out of her and made her writhe inside when she remembered how she'd promised Reece she wouldn't go all gooey-eyed on him. Swallowing a groan, she eased out from under the heavy leg thrown across both of hers and groped for her panties.

What *was* it about Chalo Canyon that clouded her thinking, made her so damned vulnerable to a handsome face?

No, not just a handsome face. As Reece had so forcefully reminded her, he wasn't Jamie Chavez. Like she needed a reminder! Reece Henderson didn't operate on the same plane, or even in the same sphere as the careless, casual Jamie.

Resolutely she pulled on her wrinkled top. When her head pushed through the neck opening, she found Reece with his hands hooked comfortably under his neck, his eyes on her breasts, and a sexy smile on his lips. As if remembering the pleasure they'd experienced at the touch of those lips, her nipples peaked.

For heaven's sake! One look from the man and she was ready to throw herself on top of him again and devour him whole. So much for her promise not to make a fool of herself!

"The storm's passed," she muttered, embarrassed by her body's involuntary reaction.

"I see."

Yanking down the hem of her tank top, she pointed out more of the obvious. "It's late. The moon's up."

He nodded solemnly.

A little desperate, she tugged her shorts from under his hip. "At least we'll have some light for the trek out of the canyon."

"You don't have to worry, Sydney. I'll get you home safely...if and when you're ready to leave."

She bit down on her lower lip, both seduced and appalled at the invitation in his tanned-leather voice. She couldn't blame him for wanting seconds. She wanted them, too. So badly her stomach curled in on itself. And she couldn't blame anyone but herself for that lazy, predatory gleam in his eyes. She'd set this whole situation up, promised him a roll in the hay— or in this case, a roll on the rocks—with no strings attached.

"I'm not worried," she assured him. "I just want to take advantage of this glorious moonlight to shoot a few exterior angles."

His sexy little smile faded at her swift transition from passionate lover to equally passionate movie-maker.

"I just hope Zack left some of the high-speed

film,'' she added under her breath, scrambling into her shorts with more haste than dignity.

"Wait a minute. We have to talk."

"No, we don't." She summoned what was probably the world's most insipid smile. "We talked before I jumped your bones, remember? I promised you I wouldn't make the same mistake I made ten years ago, and I won't."

He dragged on his jeans. "Dammit, Sydney..."

"It's okay." She backed away, groping behind her for the opening in the stone that formed the door. "I'm not expecting any declarations of undying love, and I certainly won't lay any on you."

On that firm note, she ducked under the stone lintel and disappeared through the doorway, leaving Reece to glower at the dark rectangle. Five minutes ago he'd roused from a lazy state of satisfaction to the glorious sight of Sydney nearly naked, her mouth still swollen from his kiss and her eyes filled with confusion as she tried to sort out the ramifications of what they'd just shared.

Reece could appreciate her confusion. He was tasting its sharp tang himself. He'd pulled Sydney into his arms with only a vague, hazy worry about where they'd go from here, but now...

Now, what?

Now he wanted her even more fiercely than he had an hour ago. He'd just admitted it to himself when she'd brushed him off with that casual assurance that she wouldn't fall in love with him. Somehow, that wasn't what he wanted to hear right now. Casual didn't come close to describing his feelings for Sydney Scott at this moment.

He yanked on his clothes, trying to catalogue and arrange the sensations she evoked in him in ascending order of importance.

Irritation. Lust. Admiration. Worry.

Especially worry.

His face grim, he yanked on his shirt and ducked through the low door to retrace his steps through the dark, winding ruins. Pushing upright outside the last building, he scanned the cave's mouth.

Silhouetted against a midnight-blue sky studded with thousands of stars, Sydney picked her way through the ruins toward the ladder. Reece reached her just in time to bar her descent.

"We need to talk. *Not* about what just happened between us," he added quickly when she opened her mouth to give him what he guessed would be another of her thanks-it-was-fun-and-I'll-call-you-sometime speeches. "We'll discuss that later. Before we do, I need to tell you what brought me into the canyon tonight."

So much for her fatal attraction, Sydney thought wryly. She'd gotten so caught up in the moment...and in his arms...that she hadn't even questioned Reece's unexpected appearance at the ruins.

"Did you get the results back on your computer simulations?" she asked, cutting to what she assumed was the key issue.

His mouth settled into a tight line. "Yes, I did."

"Not good?"

"Let's just say they weren't what I expected. We start blasting tomorrow. You won't be able to access this part of the canyon for the next couple of days."

She bit back her instinctive protest. She'd agreed

to work around his schedule. But two days! Two precious days in which she'd planned to retake the footage lost to the slasher.

Her mind raced. She could still make her deadline. She'd do the interviews in town, rerecord Henry's stories. Maybe go over the stock tapes on the Anasazis she'd purchased from the State Historical Archives to see how and where she could flesh out her own footage. Absorbed in her mental calculations, she almost missed Reece's next comment.

"I talked to Martinez this afternoon. Out on Canyon Rim Road, at the spot where you drove over the cliff."

No one seemed to make the fine distinctions she did about that particular incident. She folded her arms, determined to set the record straight once and for all.

"Swerving to avoid a rock in the road and having the road crumble beneath you is *not* the same as driving over a cliff."

"That's true," Reece admitted.

She barely had time to savor her little victory in the war of words before the ground started to crumble beneath her feet again.

"Some people are questioning how that rock got into the road," he said slowly.

Her arms dropped. "Like who, for instance?"

"Like me."

"I thought…" Reeling, Sydney struggled to grasp the implications of that terse reply. "I assumed—"

Oh, God! She'd assumed that slab of limestone had simply fallen from the cliff beside the road, an accidental product of rain and the eroding wind that whistled through the canyon.

"Are you saying someone pushed that rock into the road deliberately? Someone who knew I'd be driving along that stretch of the canyon after dark?"

"I'm saying it's possible." He kept his eyes on hers, as if to gauge her reaction. "I found some marks on the stone that could have been made by a chisel."

"A chisel," Sydney echoed, feeling sick.

"Or by another falling rock," he added sharply. "Martinez shipped a piece of it to a metallurgy lab in Tucson. We should hear from them within a day or two."

Wrapping her arms around her waist, she fought the sudden chills that started at her fingertips and worked their way inward toward her heart.

"Sebastian."

A shiver danced like a nervous spider down her back.

Seeing the shudder, Reece felt his jaw tighten in its socket. He hated scaring her like this, hated seeing that grim, determined look in her eyes.

Restraining the urge to fold her into his arms, he was obligated to repeat the deputy's caution. "As of this point, there's no proof that any of the Chavez family was involved in either your accident or the malicious destruction of your cassettes."

"It was Sebastian."

Silently Reece could only agree with her low, re-verberating assertion. Arlene might have slashed her perceived rival's tapes out of desperation, but only Sebastian possessed the strength or the ruthlessness to arrange such a clever and convenient obstacle on Canyon Rim Road.

If it was arranged.

They wouldn't know for a few days, Reece reminded himself. In the meantime he and Henry would keep Sydney and her crew under close surveillance. Very close surveillance.

And Reece would take the night shift.

The quiet that stretched between him and Sydney during the drive back to town told Reece that he'd be keeping watch over her tonight from a distance. The mind-shattering intimacy they'd shared during that hour in the cave dissipated a little more with every mile. By the time he pulled into the Lone Eagle Motel's gravel parking lot, a quiet, withdrawn woman had completely effaced the one who'd shattered into a million pieces in his arms.

Reece missed her...more than he was ready to admit.

They had just climbed out of the Jeep when a door banged open and Zack sauntered out.

"Where you been, boss? I was, like, getting worried."

"We got caught by the storm."

The kid's gaze drifted from Sydney's tangled hair to Reece's half-buttoned shirt. A smirk tilted down the corners of his mouth.

"Musta been some storm."

"It was."

She shoved her key in the lock and pushed open the door of her room. Reece brushed past her. A quick search of the bedroom and the bathroom beyond revealed no destruction or uninvited guests. Satisfied, he went back outside to unload the Jeep.

"Here, I'll take those," she said.

Lifting the cases from his hands, she muttered a stiff good-night. A moment later the door banged in his face.

Reece stood on the stoop, debating whether he should pound on the door and inform Ms. Scott that they still had unfinished business to discuss or just open the blasted thing and walk in. He didn't want to leave her alone and shaken like this. Hell, he might as well admit it. He didn't want to leave her at all.

What he wanted was Sydney. Any way he could have her. The truth hit him right between the eyes just seconds before Zack hit him right between the shoulder blades. The friendly thump carried more force than the kid's thin frame and lank manner would suggest he possessed.

"You look like you could use a beer. I know I could. I'll keep you company if you'll buy."

Reece slanted him an assessing look. "Are you old enough to drink? Legally?"

"I'm old enough to do anything legally. It's the illegal stuff that gets me in trouble. Hey, man," he added when his prospective drinking companion didn't jump at the offer, "I'm twenty-five and then some. Ask Lula if you don't believe me. She's already carded me twice."

"Once wasn't enough?"

"She had a few doubts about my driver's license the first time I showed it to her," he admitted. "On closer examination, she finally decided that geek with the glasses and the greased-down hair was really me." He palmed his green-tinted spikes. "Took me a while to convince her that people do change over the years."

Years, hell. Reece had changed profoundly in the past few hours. He just wasn't sure how, yet.

He fell in beside the kid, too edgy and wired to hit the sack. He could see the entire motel courtyard from the café. He'd have a beer, draw the kid out, maybe learn a little about the prickly woman who'd just slammed the door in his face.

What he learned about Sydney went down as easily as the beers...at first.

"She's one of the best," Zack said sometime later, his slang giving way to a quiet intensity. "We studied her *Buccaneers* at UCLA. That was one of her first projects for The History Channel. It's a classic, a superb blending of historical fact and popular lore about the pirates who pillaged the seas. She completely debunked those scumbags' romantic image without destroying the myths that surround them. The way she fed those black-and-white stills into her color footage..." He shook his head, his face a study in awe and envy. "You ought to see it."

"I have. I just didn't know it was hers."

"She did that one on her own, with only a mini-cam and rented stills."

"Sounds like she's come a long way." Reece swirled his beer, thinking of the woman who'd left Chalo Canyon in disgrace and come back an accomplished, accredited filmmaker. "Now she owns her own studio."

"Almost owns her own studio," Zack corrected with a shrug. "She's put everything she has into it.

Everything she had left after her dad's hospital bills, anyway. She's got to wrap this project and produce *The Weeping Woman of Chalo Canyon* as promised or she'll lose the projected broadcast date, not to mention a chance at another Oscar nomination this cycle. Even worse,'' he said morosely, staring down at the amber dregs in his glass, ''she'll sacrifice her dream.''

''What dream?''

The kid tipped him a curious glance. ''She didn't tell you? I'm not surprised. Sydney's still tight about her father and what this project meant to him. To them both. She'll do anything to wrap it. Anything.''

The look in the kid's eyes went from curious to speculative and stayed that way just long enough to plant an ugly little doubt in Reece's mind. He shoved it out immediately. ''Anything'' did *not* include flashing ten-megawatt smiles at the chief engineer to assure access to the dam site...much less seducing him. His insides were still tight with the memory of those hours in the cave, when Zack pushed his chair away from the table.

''I'd better zone out. No doubt Syd will want us all up and on our way to the canyon by dawn.''

Reece didn't say anything. It wasn't his place to inform Sydney's crew that they wouldn't be shooting on-site tomorrow. She'd advise them of the change in locale in her own time, her own way.

With a nod to Lula, Zack sauntered out. A few moments later, the generous-hipped waitress plopped down in the vacated chair. A frown creased her broad face.

"What's this I hear 'bout Sydney's accident bein' no accident?"

Beer sloshed over the rim of the glass as Reece shot upright. "How did you hear about that?"

The café's proprietress waved a plump hand, as if the mechanics of her widespread communications network weren't important, only its accuracy. "Arlene came into town this morning, looking as shook up as I've ever seen her. I made her guzzle some coffee and a piece of pie." Lula's head wagged. "That woman's gonna dry up and blow away if she doesn't watch herself. I've tried to tell her staying skinny as a bag of bones won't keep Jamie if he's a mind to stray, but...well..."

With a shrug of her rounded shoulders, she got back to the real meat of the matter. "While Arlene was here, she let drop 'bout Joe Martinez coming out to the ranch and askin' for alibis."

Let drop, his left foot! Reece suspected Lula pried the information out of Arlene with the same ruthlessness Torquemada extracted confessions from the victims of the Spanish Inquisition.

The café operator's brown eyes fixed on Reece. "I've known Sebastian Chavez a long time. Both Martha and I had our eye on him before he married that silly piece of fluff who ran off and left him with a baby to raise. He's hard and he's proud and he dotes on that boy."

Reece didn't mention the fact that the "boy" was now a man, full grown and more than capable of making his own decisions.

"Hard and proud enough to shame the nineteen-year-old girl he didn't think was good enough for his son into leaving town?'' he asked.

"And then some.''

"Hard enough to arrange her death when she came back ten years later and threatened to destroy his family?''

Lula scratched the plastic tablecloth with a short, stubby finger. Her brown eyes were grave when she met Reece's gaze.

"There's some 'round here that might think so.''

He leaned forward, his beer glass forgotten. "What about you? What do you think?''

"I think I'll sleep better now that I've had new dead bolts put on the door to Sydney's unit.'' The seriousness in her face eased into a knowing smirk. "Thought you might want to know that, since you seem to have taken such a shine to that woman. What were you two doin' out at the ruins so long, anyway?''

Sydney had already provided the residents of Chalo Canyon with enough gossip to last a lifetime. Reece wasn't about to give them more.

"Waiting out the storm.''

Lula's keen brown eyes roamed his face and the hair Reece hadn't taken the time to comb.

"If you say so.''

Lifting her bulk from the chair, she dug into her pocket. A room key landed on the table with a little jangle of metal on plastic.

"Henry Three Pines stopped by earlier and asked Martha to move you into Unit Eleven. He seems to think you wanted to stay close to Sydney. Real close. We've already moved your gear.''

Reece closed his fist over the key. "Thanks."

"It connects to Unit Twelve." Her face deliberately bland, Lula started back to the kitchen. "The door locks on both sides."

Chapter 11

Squeaky clean and feeling almost human after a long, stinging shower, Sydney wrapped herself in one of the Lone Eagle Motel's skimpy bath towels and tucked the edges tightly around her breasts. Steam filled the tiny bathroom, fogging the glass surfaces. Slowly, her mind drifting, she rubbed a clear space on the mirror, turned on the taps and picked up her toothbrush.

Here, alone in her rented room, with only the quiet of the night outside and the rush of water through the faucets to disturb the silence, the doubts she'd held at bay during the ride into town rose up to haunt her. Maybe she should call it quits. Pack up her crew and her dreams and head back to L.A. while she still could. If Reece's suspicions proved true, and someone had really engineered that accident on Canyon Rim Road...

A shudder shook her. For a moment her hand

trembled so badly Sydney couldn't trust herself to squirt the toothpaste onto the brush. Her face looked distorted, frightened, in the dew-streaked mirror.

The image disgusted Sydney.

"You tucked your tail between your legs and scuttled away from Chalo Canyon once, girl. You're not running again." Her chin came up. "Sebastian Chavez is a tough old buzzard, but you're tougher."

A lot tougher. After watching her father die by painful degrees, she could handle anything that either of the Chavez men threw at her.

That fierce advice to herself was still ringing in her ears when she walked into the bedroom a few moments later, wrapped in her towel. Without that infusion of spunk and determination, the faint, almost inaudible snick of the lock on the connecting doors might have sent her terrified into the night. Instead, the tiny sound and an accompanying surreptitious twist of the round door knob fired a surge of fury.

"Bastard," she hissed, her heart jackhammering under the thin shield of cotton. "You're not getting in...or out...without a few lumps this time."

Her bare feet flying over the pea-green shag, Sydney rushed across the room to dig through the equipment piled beside the front door. Battle fever pulsed through her blood as her fist closed around a telescoped tripod.

She swished the heavy stand through the air twice, testing its weight and balance, and was back at the door within seconds. Attack, Sydney remembered from the innumerable John Wayne war movies she'd watched with her father, was always the best defense.

Positioning herself so the door would screen her when it opened, she hefted the tripod in one hand

and reached out with another. With a quick twist of the dead bolt, a hard yank on the doorknob, and a vicious swing, Sydney let fly.

"What the...?"

The would-be intruder ducked just in time. The tripod missed his head by inches and crashed into the door frame, gouging out great chunks of the wood. At the impact, shock waves eddied up Sydney's arm. She had already pulled back for another swing before she recognized the astonished man who shot up a hand and grabbed her weapon.

"Reece!" Outraged and relieved, she screeched at him. "You scared the hell out of me!"

"Yeah, well, you've just taken a year off my life span." His narrowed gaze swept her bare flesh. "Maybe two."

Releasing her grip on the tripod, she snatched at the towel that had worked loose in the near melee.

"What are you doing?" she demanded, quivering with indignation.

"I was testing the locks between our rooms." He hefted the tripod, eyeing it with a scowl. "Care to tell me what in blue blazes you intended to accomplish with this?"

"I *intended* to bash your head in. I'll do it, too, if you ever scare me like that again."

"I thought you were in the bathroom," he said shortly, obviously as pumped by the near miss as she was.

"I was." Frowning, she caught a glimpse of the clothing hung neatly in the room's small closet. "I thought this unit was empty."

"I just moved in."

Sydney's gaze whipped back to his. He'd moved

in next to her? Only a connecting door away? The implications sent a wave of heat through her body. Did he think that she wanted to pick up where they'd left off this afternoon? More to the point, did she?

"I'm a light sleeper," he said, cutting into her chaotic thoughts. "I thought you might want someone close at hand in case you get any more unwanted visitors."

"Oh."

The idea of Reece bedding down right next door, only a few feet away, rattled her all the way down to her toes. Almost as much as the idea that he'd switched rooms to keep watch over her.

She'd been on her own for so long, been strong for herself and her father for so long, that Sydney couldn't decide how to respond to Reece's unexpected protective streak. Not that she trusted herself to say anything coherent at this moment.

It had just sunk in that he wasn't wearing much more than she was.

Bare-chested, barefoot, his jeans slung low on his hips, he radiated even more of the potent masculinity that had melted her bones in the cave. Remembering the way she'd fallen all over him only a few hours ago, Sydney flushed.

"Reece, about what happened at the ruins..."

"When you came apart in my arms, you mean?"

Her flush deepened. "As I recall, we both did a little coming apart."

"So we did."

"But I don't... You don't..."

He let her stumble for a moment or two before he asked with a curious bite to his voice, "Is this another one of your attempts to reassure me that you have no intention of falling for me?"

"Something like that."

"Save the speech, Sydney." He stepped through the opened doorway, his eyes dark behind his black lashes. "What happened this afternoon confused the heck out of me, too, but I'm not making any promises."

Under the thin cotton towel, her heart did a number on her ribs. She held her breath as he lifted a hand to tip her face to his.

"I don't know where we go from here," he said gruffly, "but I'm willing to explore the possibilities."

"You understand the risk? The last time I got involved with a man in Chalo Canyon, the whole town got involved with me."

Her attempt at humor went wide of the mark. Reece didn't crack a smile.

"I told you, I'm not Jamie Chavez."

"I do believe you mentioned that already."

"I want to make sure we're clear on that point."

"We are," she breathed. "Very clear."

Bound and blindfolded, Sydney couldn't confuse this man with Jamie or anyone else. His scent, his touch, the unconscious air of authority he carried like a second shadow set him apart.

"And this isn't ten years ago," he told her fiercely. "You're not alone in this."

"In what, Reece?"

He stared down at her, his rugged features set. "Damned if I know."

The muttered reply formed a tight band around Sydney's chest. To tell the truth, she had no idea where the sparks that sizzled under her skin every time he touched her would lead them, either. Feeling slightly overwhelmed by all that had happened between them in such a short time, she tried for a smile.

"Let's just take it a day at a time."

Reece didn't answer for a moment. He couldn't. His entire body had gone hard at the thought of tumbling her back on the chenille spread, kissing that full mouth and taut body until they both shot to the stars again.

The purple shadows under her eyes put the brakes on his rampaging need. She'd gotten up before dawn, he remembered. He remembered, too, how she'd fallen asleep in his arms during the storm.

"One day at a time," he echoed slowly. "Starting tomorrow."

"Starting tomorrow," she agreed, coming up on tiptoe to seal the bargain with a brush of her lips against his. He shuddered at the featherlight touch.

"Reece...?"

"Don't worry," he half groaned, then managed a grin. "I'm a man of my word. We'll take this slow."

Even if it killed him.

He shut the door between their rooms a moment later, wondering just what in God's name they were starting...and how they'd finish.

Reece woke well before dawn, driven by the realization that this day would see the start of more than a hazy, yet-to-be-defined relationship with Sydney Scott.

The repair project he'd sweated over for more than ten months was about to enter its most critical phase. The contractor and his crew would begin placing the small, densely packed charges this morning. If all went as planned, the weakened quadrant of the inner wall would be exposed by afternoon. For the first time, Reece would see the stress fractures with his own eyes.

He showered and slathered on shaving cream, listening for sounds that would indicate Sydney was awake. Briefly he toyed with the idea of going down to the café for coffee. He could bring some back for her. Serve it to her in bed. Join her under the covers for a few minutes.

Yeah, right. As if he could climb in and out of bed with her in less than an hour or two. Or three.

Or ever.

The razor slipped down his chin, taking a patch of skin with it.

"Ouch!"

Grabbing a wad of toilet tissue, Reece dabbed at the cut. The thing wouldn't stop bleeding. He walked out into the sharp, predawn chill sometime later sporting a crusted bit of toilet paper on his chin.

Henry Three Pines drove up in his rickety pickup while the dam crew was still assembling. His eyes were almost lost under wrinkled folds of lid, but Reece trusted the man's eyesight and instinct.

"You'll stay with her?"

"She is my friend and the daughter of my friend. I will stay with her."

Reece threw a quick glance at the door to Unit Twelve. "I'll get back as soon as I can tonight. We'll be blasting today, so it may be late," he warned.

"I will stay with her."

The Hopi headman was in the café when Sydney strolled out of her room an hour later, her arms filled with a load of equipment. She spotted him through the brightly lit glass, dumped her load in the van and joined him for a quick cup of coffee.

"What do we shoot today?" he asked when she'd settled beside him with a steaming mug.

"Local interviews. I want to get a feel for the people who now inhabit the land of the Ancient Ones. Hopefully I'll also get them talking about the Weeping Woman." She aimed a smile at the woman busy wiping down the counter. "I'll tape Lula and Martha when we get back this evening, after the supper rush."

Henry's wrinkled face folded into a smile. "They would never forgive you if you did not include them in this film you make."

"I know."

Sighing, Sydney sipped her coffee. She'd conducted hundreds of interviews over the years. The hardest ones were with friends and acquaintances.

Good documentarians constructed an invisible wall between their crews and the subjects. The *really* good ones maintained that wall throughout the entire interview process. The object was to avoid influencing the subjects' behavior or nudging them too hard down the paths you hoped they would go.

That could get a little difficult when said subjects had known you all your life.

"I also want to interview Mrs. Brent. Does she still have her 'visions'?"

"Whenever the moon is full."

Henry's own culture was too steeped in spiritualism and kachinas to ridicule the woman half the town referred to as Crazy Lady Brent. The eccentric recluse had terrified and totally intrigued the wide-eyed, nine-year-old Sydney the first time they'd come face-to-face during one of Mrs. Brent's lonely walks across the mesa. If anyone could produce the eerie feel Sydney wanted for her film, the gray-haired widow could. The trick would be to get her to recount some of the tales about the Weeping Woman of Chalo Canyon in front of a camera.

"I've got Buck Sanders and Joe Smallwood lined up this morning," she told Henry, referring to two local ranchers. "Mrs. Brent said we could come out to her place after lunch. I'll shoot the supper crowd at the café before we set up for Lula and Martha."

"We'll be busy," Henry commented with a smile.

"We will."

Impatient now to get to work, Sydney roused her crew. She used the drive out to Buck Sanders's isolated ranchero to review her notes for the interview. Like Henry, Buck was a member of the Hopi tribe and could speak authoritatively on the farming and irrigation techniques their people had learned or stolen from the ancient Anasazi. That would fit right in with a central theme of Sydney's documentary, which was to show the blending of ancient ways into modern culture as well as the mix of reality into myth.

Under other circumstances, she would have begged an interview with Sebastian Chavez. His family had lived in the Chalo Canyon area for as long as anyone could remember. The proud blood of the Spanish and equally proud blood of the Hopi mingled in his veins. With his white hair, hawk's beak of a nose and haughty bearing, he made the kind of visual impact that ordinarily made Sydney's fingers itch for a camera.

Now, just the thought of capturing him on videotape raised goose bumps.

Could he hate her so much? Fear her so much? Had he tumbled that slab of rock into Canyon Rim Road in a deliberate attempt to harm her?

The questions haunted Sydney as Henry guided her and her crew over narrow, dusty back roads. Finally Buck Sanders's place came into view. Tucked under an overhang of granite, the adobe ranch house looked exactly like what it was—a small, working homestead. They'd shoot outside, Sydney decided. Take advantage of the natural light and great visuals.

She made it a point to conduct interviews on the subject's home ground whenever possible. She wanted them to feel comfortable, without the constraints that too often inhibited them in a studio or an artificial set. That meant lugging extra lighting from location to location, of course, but the results generally justified the extra effort.

Generally.

Today might prove the exception. Despite Sydney's best efforts to put the taciturn Buck Sanders at ease, he couldn't relax. He kept a death grip on his coffee cup, looked straight at Sydney instead of the camera, and waited for her questions, which he answered with as few words as possible. The result was a stiff, stilted interview and several hundred wasted feet of videotape.

She had better luck with Joe Smallwood. Bright-eyed and leathery from his years under the Arizona sun, he spat out a chaw and waxed eloquent about ter from upriver to the mesa above the ruins more than a thousand years ago.

"Those ditches run some twenty, thirty miles," he ruminated in his tobacco-roughened caw. "Folks 'round here were still using stretches of 'em before the Chalo River dam went in."

She'd have to get some footage of the dam, Sydney thought as she and her crew drove to the next location. Maybe she'd tie the massive structure to both the drowning of the Anasazi village and the salvation of the farmers who came after them. The Bureau of Reclamation could probably dig some stock footage of the dam's construction out of its archives for her.

Or...

She could ask Reece for a private tour of the structure. That would give her the opportunity to observe him in action, maybe help her understand this project that consumed him almost as fiercely as Sydney's did her. She would talk to him tonight, she thought with a shiver of anticipation, about shooting some footage at the dam.

Among other things.

It took a surprising effort of will to blank those other things out of her mind and prepare for the afternoon's interview. Luckily the hollow-cheeked retired schoolteacher-turned-eccentric needed little prompting to talk about the Weeping Woman. Laura Brent closed her eyes, transporting herself from a living room crowded with knickknacks and photographs, not to mention floodlights, cameras and sound equipment, to a place inhabited only by her imagination.

"I hear her often," she murmured. "Whenever the

love. Some say she was Zuni, stolen away from her home to the north. Yet the words, the lament, are Hopi.''

Her voice rose, thinned.

"Aiiiiiii. Eee-aiiiii."

It was the cry of the wind, the wail of a desperate woman. With all her heart, Sydney prayed Albert was getting this.

"I heard her the week after I lost my husband to a perforated ulcer," Laura said sadly, as if the long-ago event had happened just yesterday. "She cried for me."

"This is good," Albert muttered as he played with the levers and dials on his unit. "This is good."

Better than good, Sydney thought exultantly. It was great. The sound take echoed the one they'd recorded in the canyon the other night with uncanny precision. During the postproduction editing process, Sydney would cut from Brent's bright living room to the dark cave. Juxtapose the modern woman with the ancient one. Synthesize recent grief with ancient heartbreak.

She was still on a high from the great visuals and audio when the crew set up in the motel's lobby for the interview with the Jenkins sisters later that evening. The two women turned out for the shoot in their Sunday best. Adorned in squash-blossom necklaces and elaborate earrings, they made a study in contrasts. Through the camera lens, Lula came across as plump, dark-eyed and ready to dish out a healthy dose of laughter. Martha appeared thin, nervous and twittery.

While Albert ran sound checks and Tish adjusted

They talked about the weather and the unseasonable rain, about business at the motel, about the ingredients in Lula's own brand of steak marinade. Sydney didn't hesitate to use audiotape lavishly in these preinterview sessions. Often she got plenty of good sound to use as off-camera fill if the on-camera interview went badly.

When she sensed the sisters were comfortable, she surreptitiously signaled Tish to start shooting. Caught up in their dialogue, Lula and Martha didn't realize they were being recorded on videotape. Slowly, imperceptibly, Sydney withdrew behind the glass shield that separated her from her subjects. Sitting off to one side, content behind her invisible wall, she listened while they poured out tales composed of equal parts gossip, personal accounts and dubious historical fact. Hands moving, heads nodding, they spoke of their ancestors. Of the town of Chalo Canyon. Of the Weeping Woman.

Following their cue, Sydney eased into her role as interviewer for a moment. "Do you remember when you first heard about the legend?"

Martha cocked her head. "Seems like I've heard about the Weeping Woman all my life."

"All your life? From the time you were a small child?"

"Well, I'll have to think about that...."

Lula jumped in at this point. "I don't! I know the very day I first heard about the Weeping Woman. It was thirty-six years ago."

"How the heck can you remember that?" her sister demanded. "You can't even remember to let the dog out in the morning."

With that somewhat confusing but firm declaration, the younger Jenkins sister launched into her tale.

"Sebastian told me the story one night when he stopped in for a beer, 'bout six months after his wife ran off. He was red-eyed with fatigue and with carin' for his ranch and the boy. We talked about cattle prices and the hay crop and the fierce wind that whistled through the canyon. He went all bitter and hard when I said it sounded like a woman wailing, but before he left the café he unbent enough to pass on the story of the Anasazi woman that his grandfather had told him."

Sydney leaned forward, her heart pounding. Sebastian was the original source of the legend? Damn, she wished she could interview him.

"I sure never wanted to trek down to the ruins again after he told me how that poor woman jumped out of the stone tower," Lula added, grimacing. "Then the dam went in, the canyon flooded, and the Weeping Woman became part of local lore."

Martha appeared struck by her sister's account. "You know, I believe you're right."

"I know I'm right. I always am."

"Ha!" The elder Miss Jenkins shattered the glass wall by appealing directly to Sydney. "Ask her who was right about that Buick she insisted we buy? The thing ended up in the junkyard less than a year after we drove it off the lot down in Phoenix."

"If you'd ever learned how to drive," her loving sister retorted, "it would have lasted a sight longer."

Wisely, Sydney stayed out of the heated debate that followed. She terminated the interview some

kinses were still arguing over who ran the Buick into
the ground when the crew packed up their equipment
and left.

Agreeably tired from the long day, Sydney trailed
out of the lobby a moment later. She found Henry
outside under the café's awning, with his chair tipped
against the motel wall and his face turned up to the
darkening sky.

"Thanks for coming with us today," she told him
with a grateful smile. "I doubt if I could have found
Buck's ranch on my own."

"You would've found it, Little Squirrel." He
pushed to his feet. "You have the heart to always
find your way. So," he added, glancing over her
shoulder, "does he."

Sydney spun around. When she spotted Reece
climbing out of his Jeep, his hair and eyebrows
coated with a whitish dust, the heart Henry had just
referred to started knocking against her ribs.

Reece didn't notice her and Henry under the awning. His stride long and swift, he headed toward his
room.

After a quick goodbye to Henry, Sydney did the
same.

Chapter 12

Reece closed his room door behind him, fully intending to honor his promise to Sydney to take things slow.

He'd spent the past fifteen hours struggling to douse the simmering heat that rose under his skin whenever she slipped into his thoughts. With the noise and distraction that came with blasting away three thousand cubic yards of concrete, he'd pretty much managed to keep her firmly at the back of his mind.

Gritty and bone-weary after all those hours in the heat and the sun, he'd climbed into his Jeep for the long drive back to town. Only minutes after the majestic curve of the dam disappeared from the rearview mirror, Sydney had pushed right to the forefront of Reece's worries.

Deputy Sheriff Martinez had called earlier to confirm that his people had delivered the sample slab of sandstone to the Department of Mine Engineering's metallurgy lab in Tucson. Reece himself had contacted Jan Kingsley, who promised to get the sample under the electron microscope within the next twenty-four hours.

In the meantime...

Reece smiled grimly, crinkling the grit at the corners of his eyes. In the meantime, he and Sydney would slow down, temper the heat that sizzled between them, find the balance between her schedule demands and his. Learn more about each other. He'd take time to understand the artistic vision that took her down into a canyon with thirty pounds of equipment on her back, maybe even share a few more laws of physics with her.

Like the inclined plane.

And the simple lever.

Groaning, Reece banished the instant, erotic image of her inclined and him levering. How in blazes he was going to manage slow escaped him at this moment, when all he could think about was a hot shower, a cold drink, and Sydney in his arms.

That question came to the fore when she pounded on the connecting door between their rooms just moments later. She smiled up at him, her face almost as dusty as his, her hair a wind-tossed mass of mink under a red L.A. Dodgers ball cap.

Instantly, his priorities rearranged themselves. To hell with the cold beer, he decided on a surge of need. It would probably just mix with all the dust he'd swallowed today and harden into concrete in his stomach. And the hot shower could wait. The feel of this woman in his arms couldn't. Not for long, anyway. Particularly when her smile delivered the same wallop as the roughhouse punches he and his brothers used to lay on each other.

"Hi."

The simple greeting contracted Reece's stomach. "Hi."

"How did it go today?"

"We hit the inner core in the lower-right quadrant."

"Is that good?"

He grinned. "Very good. We expected that it would take at least two days to expose the core, but the contractor had a real pro setting the charges."

"So they're done blasting?"

"Looks like it."

He knew what was coming before she slanted him a quick, speculative look.

"Does that mean I can take my crew back down to the ruins tomorrow?"

Reece hesitated, reluctant to break the unwelcome news that more violent thunderstorms were headed their way. The Upper Colorado region had already received record rainfalls for the year. From all indications, the Lower Colorado basin would soon do the same.

Spurred by the latest forecasts, the subcontractor had performed the near impossible and finished the blasting in a single day. Now all Reece had to worry about was the possibility of flash floods raging through the canyon and taking out his crippled dam, not to mention Sydney and her crew.

"Why don't we talk about schedules after I clean up?" he suggested.

She eyed him suspiciously, probably guessing that he was the bearer of bad news, but didn't push it. "Okay by me. I'll get a couple of beers from the café. You look like you could use something cold and wet."

Just in time, Reece bit back the observation that he was far more interested in something warm and wet. Like her lips. Or the curve of her neck. Or any part of her she wanted to make available.

"You," he announced instead, sliding a palm around her nape, "are a woman of remarkable intelligence and perception."

"You've noticed that, have you?"

Her smug little smile almost destroyed what was left of his control. It took a severe effort of will to keep the pacing deliberate, the touch light.

Just one taste, he told himself as he lowered his head. A small sampling.

The moment his lips covered hers, Reece knew one sampling wouldn't be enough. She smelled of wind and woman, of sunshine and Lula's special brew of supercharged coffee. Her mouth shaped instantly to his, as though she'd learned the angle of his jaw, the contours of his face.

Despite his clamoring body's protest, Reece managed to keep to just the one kiss. When he pulled back, she gave a shaky little laugh.

"You taste like cement."

He cocked a brow. "Have you ever tasted cement before?"

"No, but there's a first time for everything."

"So they say."

The small blue vein in her throat drew both his gaze and his touch. He edged his thumb down the faint line, felt her pulse fluttering under his thumb pad.

"Maybe they're right," he murmured.

This tight, driving need was definitely a first for Reece. Lying awake, listening to the whistle of the wind last night, he'd gone over every minute of those hours in the ruins. By the time he'd dragged himself out of bed, he'd almost been convinced that he'd imagined his grinding need. That Sydney hadn't arched under him and exploded in that shattering release.

Now he knew he hadn't imagined anything. Her blood pulsed under his thumb. Her skin felt like satin under his touch. God, he wanted her. Needed her the way a chocaholic needed his sweet, dark fix. The hours he'd spent with her had drowned his doubts, his half-formed, almost subconscious disdain for the woman everyone in Chalo Canyon had painted as a homewrecker.

An engineer down to his steel-toed boots, he was still trying to measure her impact on his internal Richter scale when she backed away. To Reece's immense satisfaction, her breath came as hard and fast as his.

"I'll...I'll get the drinks," she gasped. "Pound on the door when you're ready."

He was ready, more than ready, even before he stepped into a cool, stinging shower. *Slow,* he reiterated through gritted teeth. They were going to go slow. Even if it crippled him, which seemed a definite possibility at this point.

He soon discovered that Sydney's definition of *slow* differed considerably from his. She answered his knock fifteen minutes later with a dew-streaked bottle and a kiss that completely destroyed the effect of his cold shower.

Twenty minutes later they tumbled onto her bed, naked and panting.

"I thought about you all day," she admitted between hard, hungry kisses. "You got in the way of my shoot."

Since her tongue was busy exploring his ear at that point, Reece ignored the faint but unmistakable accusation.

"I thought about you, too, between detonations."

"You did, huh?" Her breath fanned his ear, hot, damp, incredibly arousing. "Why don't we see what we can do to set off a few more explosive charges?"

Her tongue got busier. Instantly Reece got harder. Groaning, he hunched a shoulder. Wrapping both hands around her waist, he slid her down a few inches. The friction of her breasts on his chest, her hips on his pelvis, set off more than just a *few* explosions. The ache that had started low in Reece's belly grew hotter, tighter, wilder with each taste, each teasing, wondering touch.

In the dimness of the ruins yesterday, she'd set him on fire. In the puddle of light thrown by the lamp beside the bed, she was gloriously greedy in her want, spectacularly generous in her giving. He dug his hands in the dark hair that spilled over her shoulders, lost himself in the damp, smooth heat of her mouth.

They were both slick with sweat when Sydney slid a leg over his and rose up on her knees. Yesterday he'd pleasured her so thoroughly, so skillfully. Today, the urge to do the same brought her upright, her hands on her thighs, her hips straddling his.

Her throat closed with the sight of him stretched out beneath her, his muscled shoulders bunched and tight, his chest matted with sworls of black hair. Those lean hollows and flat planes could only come from hard labor and rigid discipline. This was no weekend jogger, no desk man with privileges at an exclusive spa. He lived as he worked, she suspected. Rigorously. Strenuously.

But it was his eyes that transfixed her. Blue, fierce with hunger, dark with anticipation as she eased onto his rigid shaft.

When they joined, he sucked in a sharp breath, holding himself still while she slid down his length. Slowly, so slowly, she lifted. Came down. Rose again.

Eyes narrowed to glittering slits, he dug his fingers into the soft flesh of her hips to guide her. His breathing grew harsh, ragged, picked up the same fast tempo as Sydney's. His hips came up to meet hers, his thighs twisted like steel under hers. She felt each slide, each thrust, each clench of her muscles and his.

"Did I say…you were a woman…of remarkable intelligence?" he rasped.

"I believe you mentioned it, yes."

"Make that…just plain…remarkable."

At the ragged edge to his voice, a thrill of feminine satisfaction pierced the silky curtain of pleasure wrapping itself around Sydney. The wanton, wicked urge to shatter Reece's control into a million tiny pieces spurred her. He looked so determined to hold back, so unused to relinquishing command of any situation.

She leaned forward, planting her hands on his shoulders to give her additional leverage. He didn't hesitate. With swift, unerring skill, he took the tantalizing target she offered. When his mouth fastened on her breast, needles of pure sensation shot from her nipple to her chest to every part of her body. Gasping, writhing where their bodies locked, Sydney rode him.

He climaxed first, shooting up under her, wrapping an arm around her waist to thrust her down, down, until she felt herself splintering.

Reece possessed, Sydney mused lazily some time later, a scent all his own—one she suspected she'd never forget.

She lay sprawled beside him, her cheek on his ribs, her nose tickled by the curly hair on his chest. With each breath, she drew in the tang of soap mixed with sweat, of healthy male. A smile tugged at her when she spotted the thin film of gray dust rimming his belly button. Evidently he'd missed that vital spot in his hurried shower.

Sydney felt the craziest urge to slide down and swipe it clean for him. Funny how she'd developed a taste for cement all of a sudden. She was contemplating what else she'd developed a taste for when a long, low growl rumbled just under her ear. She lifted her head to find Reece grinning sheepishly.

"Was that you or me?" he asked.

"You."

"Are you as hungry as I am?"

"Hungrier," she replied, matching his grin with one of her own. "I did all the work."

"Is that right?" Giving her hair a playful tug, he eased her onto her back. "Then I guess it's only fair for me to do the catering. Stay right where you are"

As if she could move! Sydney couldn't remember the last time she'd felt so totally boneless. In fact...

She couldn't remember ever feeling like this. She owed this silly, satisfied sensation in part to the burst of splendor she'd just experienced, and even more to the man now zipping up his jeans.

He dropped a kiss on her nose. "I'll be right back."

He disappeared through the connecting door. A moment later Sydney heard the door to his room slam shut. Sighing, she dragged up the spread and tucked it under her arms. Reece's scent came with the well-washed chenille, as masculine and vital as the man himself.

Okay. All right. She might as well admit it. Despite her earnest promises to the contrary, despite her determination not to make a fool of herself by tumbling head over heels in love with a man she'd met little more than a week ago, she was teetering on the edge and about to go right over.

But this time was different, her heart whispered. As Reece had pointed out so fiercely, he wasn't Jamie. He wouldn't play with her, tease her into loving him, then walk away and leave her burning with humiliation. He was like the dam he worked on. Strong. Solid. Built on a foundation of solid bedrock.

More than ever she wanted to see him in action, understand the project that took him out before dawn and brought him back late at night. They were so alike in their drive to succeed, each in their differing fields and disciplines. Eager to learn more about him and his milieu, Sydney made a mental note to ask him when he could take her down into the Chalo River Dam.

The opportunity came sooner than she expected. Cross-legged on the bed, she felt her own stomach rumbling as Reece handed her a plastic bowl brimming with pinto beans. Sopped up with huge chunks of Lula's crusty corn bread and washed down with beer, the beans made for a succulent feast. She'd gobbled down a good portion of her share when Reece brought up the forecast for tomorrow.

"There's another front moving in," he said between bites. "A big one. They're predicting severe thunderstorms for the next several days."

A big chunk of sopping corn bread froze halfway to her mouth. "Oh, no!"

"They've had some flash flooding north of here. We're watching the river levels closely." His eyes grave, he delivered the blow she'd been expecting. "It doesn't look like you should go down into the canyon for another two, possibly three days."

Sydney took a quick gulp of her beer to hide her dismay. She'd shot most of the interviews she wanted, and racked up enough exterior footage to recover from the damage done by the slasher. What she needed now were the interior shots of the ruins, particularly interiors of the stone tower the Weeping Woman of legend threw herself from.

But she couldn't afford to keep her crew twiddling their thumbs for two or three days, not at union scale. Given the prospect of additional delays, her most sensible option was to terminate the on-site shoot. She could shoot the rest of the interiors herself, as well as the final sequence when the reservoir filled and the ruins slowly disappeared beneath the water once more.

Surprisingly, the idea of finishing the takes herself didn't disturb her as much as it might have. When she'd first started out in the business, she'd shot all her own footage. She knew how to handle a mini-cam.

Added to that was the fact that she'd have time on her hands to explore Reece's world. Besides getting to know him better, she might come up with a different angle on her story, or germinate ideas for a whole new documentary.

With that thought in mind, she was able to swallow her disappointment with her beer and shift the conversation from her project to his.

"What will the rain delays do to your repairs?"

"We'll still pour. We have to. Like you, we only have a designated window of opportunity to complete this project."

"How will you keep the wet concrete from getting, er, wet?"

She braced herself for another physics lesson. Instead, she got a quick grin and a simple layman's explanation.

"We'll erect more scaffolding and use plastic sheeting to shield the fresh-poured concrete."

"When does this production begin?"

"The contractor will have a good-size fleet of cement trucks rolling in here from Phoenix in the morning."

Her ear attuned now to the voice she still wanted to capture on audiotape, Sydney detected a small sting in his reply.

"Are you being pushed?" she asked curiously.

"You might say that."

"Who by?"

He hooked a brow. "You want the whole list or the abbreviated version?"

"Start at the top and work your way down."

"At the top is the secretary of the interior, who's determined to keep his department in line with the budget cuts announced by his close buddy and golfing partner, the president."

"Of the United States?"

"Of the United States. Then there's the commissioner of the Bureau of Reclamation, who's promised his counterpart in the U.S. Fish and Wildlife Service that we'll get the reservoir refilled and restocked as soon as possible."

He stretched out on the bed, the bowl of beans balanced on his stomach. Sydney found her concentration wavering between that lean, flat plane and the list of officials watching over Reece's progress on the repairs to the Chalo River Dam.

"Let's not forget the head of the Arizona Electrical Co-Op, which purchases about half of the electricity the dam generates," he said with a grimace.

"Or the presidents of the Arizona orange and pecan growers associations, who are worried about irrigation for their commercial farms in the area. Then there's Western Region EPA office. They're monitoring the impact on the riverine environment every day we keep the dam down."

Sydney gave a long, slow whistle. "And I thought I was under pressure."

"I won't go into lurid detail about the letters we got from the Bass Anglers Sportsmen's Society, Trout Unlimited, and Outdoor America," he said dryly. "They had to cancel annual sporting events in the area. Or about my meetings with the local ranchers and farmers. Or the lectures I get every day from Lula, who reminds me every day about the business she and Martha are losing each hour the dam is down."

"Good grief! How do you sleep at night?"

"I manage." He stretched out a hand, brushed a knuckle down her cheek. "Something tells me I'll manage even better tonight."

The look in his eyes curled Sydney's toes. The corn bread fell apart in her hands, the crumbs falling unheeded to the spread.

Uh-oh! She was in trouble here. Serious trouble.

She didn't realize how much, however, until Reece took her into his arms once more. And down into his dam the next afternoon.

Chapter 13

Sydney woke the first time when Reece brushed a kiss on her cheek and told her to call him later at the dam. Prying one eye open, she peered at the clock beside the bed, saw that it was 4:20, mumbled a response, and burrowed into the covers.

She woke the second time to a distant growl of thunder. Grimacing, she lay amid the tangled sheets, listening to the rumble. Why the heck did the forecasters have to be so darned accurate in recent days, when they missed so many other predictions? Could she take another extended on-site delay?

Wide awake now, she debated once again the pros and cons of shutting down the shoot and sending the crew home early. She'd pay Albert and Tish and Katie for the sound and videotape they'd shot, as well as the standard early-wrap-up bonus. Albert had another job waiting for him, she knew, and Tish's husband would no doubt be happy to see her come striding in the door with that long-legged gait of hers. Zack... Zack, she'd start on the postproduction work. Torn, she finally admitted she had no choice. She couldn't afford to keep the crew idle.

The rain started just before nine, confirming her decision to shut down operations. Sydney spent the rest of the morning going over the postproduction schedule with Zack while Albert and Tish loaded their equipment into the van. By noon they were packed up for the hour-long drive to Phoenix, where they'd catch a flight to L.A. Several wrapped and sealed cases of videotapes would go with them. With rain splatting down on the oversize red-and-green golf umbrella Zack insisted on leaving with her, she saw the crew to the van.

"Guard those originals with your life," she warned her assistant.

"I will, I will."

"Make two copies of the window-print."

"Got it covered, Syd."

She knew he did. She'd trained him herself. Still, she preferred to personally oversee even this grunt-work part of the process. According to her best estimates, it would take Zack a day at least to make the window-print dubs...copies of the picture and sound from the original videotape with an electronic window inserted that displayed the running time in hours, minutes, seconds, and frames. Another couple of days, she knew from long experience, to label all the originals and dubs, sort through the background information they'd collected, and file and label that as well.

When those tasks were completed, Sydney could begin the arduous task of logging all the footage with the time code of each shot, scene numbers, a brief description of what happened in that scene, and notes about how the shot could be used in the final mix. Only after all that material had been entered into the computer could she use the data to begin the editing process that translated raw footage into a visual statement.

"I'll go over the dub log with you as soon as I get back," she told Zack.

"Which will be, like, when?"

"I don't know. Three days, maybe four. Everything depends on the weather."

"Su-u-u-re it does," Tish put in with a grin as she gave Sydney a quick hug and climbed into the van. "I'm leaving you the Canon two-twelve. Be sure to get some good shots of the dam, girl."

"I intend to."

"Call me if you decide to shoot that documentary on the harnessing of America's rivers."

"I will."

"And don't go, like, driving over any cliffs," Zack begged, only half in jest. "See you, Henry."

Sydney spun around, unaware that her father's old friend had lingered at the café. She'd informed him earlier that she was sending the crew back to L.A., and promised she'd call him when Reece gave her the all-clear to go down into the canyon again. Henry had simply nodded and told her he would wait for her call. She hadn't realized that he intended to do his waiting at the café.

"I have business that keeps me in town," he said simply when she asked him about it.

She was too polite to inquire into his business, but she had a good idea that it concerned her. Henry confirmed her suspicion in the next breath.

"While I'm here, I'll watch over you."

He delivered that pronouncement so calmly, so generously, that Sydney swallowed her instinctive protest.

"Thank you."

Rain dripped from the brim of Henry's felt hat onto his face. "What will you do now?"

"Now, I'm going to call Reece. He offered to take me down into the dam. If he's not up to his ears in wet cement, maybe he could give me a quick tour."

He could, he informed Sydney when she reached him a little while later. As long as she got out there within the next hour.

With Henry dozing in the Blazer's passenger seat, Sydney made tracks out to the dam. En route, she passed a convoy of dump trucks loaded with rubble heading in the opposite direction. They weren't wasting any time clearing out the debris from yesterday's blasting.

The sun poked out between patches of dark clouds just as she made the final, twisting turn down to the dam, giving her a bird's-eye view of the site. Scaffolding draped with great sheets of orange plastic covered the western quadrant, from the crest all the way down to the base. She caught only a glimpse of the gaping wound near the bottom.

Henry opted to doze in the Blazer while one of

Reece's men handed Sydney a hard hat and high rubber boots, then escorted her to the elevator that went down inside the dam to the power plant. En route, her natural curiosity prompted her to ask him about the massive crane in operation at the base of the dam.

"How did you get that monster down into the narrow gorge?"

"It was shipped here in sections and lowered piece by piece to the riverbed," her guide explained. "We're using it to clear the debris from the blasting so it doesn't block the inlet channels."

Sydney could only marvel at the detailed planning that had gone into this repair project. No wonder Reece got up before dawn and worked late at night to execute the plan, she thought as she stepped into the tiny elevator cage.

Only eight feet wide at its crest, the dam measured more than fifty-seven feet thick at its base. The deeper Sydney went into its depths, she could feel those fifty-seven feet pressing in on her.

They stepped out of the elevator in the power plant, a long, low building that housed four massive turbines. Flooded with fluorescent lighting and spotlessly clean, the cavernous chamber echoed hollowly as Sydney and her escort crossed it to join the men at the far side.

Even if she hadn't imprinted Reece's face and form on every cell in her body, she could have picked him out instantly as the person in charge. Tall, commanding, sexy as hell in his hard hat and blue workshirt with rolled-up sleeves, he listened intently to the various players before issuing a series of crisp orders.

Sydney waited quietly with her guide until he finished. Welcoming her with a smile, he introduced her to those of his crew she hadn't met, as well as to the contractor and a few of his subs.

"Hey, we've heard about you," one of the subs said. "Are you going to put us in one of your movies?"

"As a matter of fact..." Pulling the hand-held minicam out of the canvas bag slung over one shoulder, she asked Reece, "Do you mind if I shoot some footage?"

"Fine by me. If you decide to do anything with the footage, though, we'll have to run it by the Bureau's public affairs officer."

"Of course."

While the others dispersed, Sydney started having second thoughts about her request for a tour. "Are you sure you have time to show me around right now?"

"This is probably the only time I'll have for the next few days," he replied, scraping a hand across a chin that had already sprouted dark bristles. "What do you want to see first?"

"Whatever you want to show me."

"Why don't we start with the power plant, since we're right here?"

With a hand on her elbow, he guided her to the turbines. Round, green and more than two stories high, they looked like giant mandarin hats with little red buttons on top.

"When these babies are running, you can't hear

yourself think," he explained. "Combined, they generate a little over 250,000 kilowatt-hours."

Sydney looked suitably impressed.

Grinning, he put the number into perspective for her. "That's about five percent of all the power generated in the seventeen western states."

"Five percent. Got it. How do these suckers work?"

"They use the simple laws of physics."

She groaned. "Now why doesn't that surprise me?"

"They're nothing more than sophisticated water wheels," he explained, his grin widening. "Water from the reservoir flows through large tubes called penstocks under great pressure and spins the turbines. They, in turn, drive the generators which produce electricity."

Walking her past the towering turbines, he showed her where the water flowing through them would normally empty into the river below the dam. With the reservoir drained and the spillgates fully opened, the Chalo flowed through in a lazy trickle.

"Providing power was really a secondary motivation in constructing this and the other dams in the Colorado River System," Reece continued as he steered her toward a map mounted on the wall. "The primary concern was and is still flood control."

Propping a boot on a handy storage box, he swept a hand over an area encompassing the states of Colorado, Arizona and Nevada. Unobtrusively Sydney stepped back and lifted the minicam. Thank goodness for the bright lighting. With her high-speed film, she should get a usable image.

"For the millions of years the Colorado has wound its way from the Rocky Mountains to the Gulf, whole cultures have depended on it for life."

God, he looked great through the viewfinder! Tough, rugged, a man who obviously loved his work. She only hoped the echoes in this cavernous chamber didn't distort his deep, drawling narrative.

"Swollen by melting snows, the Colorado and its tributaries had a history of flooding their banks in spring and early summer. In other years, when the snow fell lighter in the northern reaches, the rivers would run dry and great droughts would occur.

"The Indians understood the annual cycles. They retreated before the floods, and when the waters subsided, they planted crops in the rich silt deposits. There wasn't much they could do to compensate for a drought, though. If it lasted too long, they moved on. Some scholars think that's what drove Anasazi out of this area."

This was good! Sydney thought excitedly. Better than good! She'd use Reece's narration as one explanation of why the Ancient Ones abandoned their homes in Chalo Canyon.

"The farmers who followed them seriously underestimated the Colorado's force. In 1905, it flooded for hundreds of miles and rampaged for nearly two years, destroying homes, livestock, whole communities. That disaster led to the establishment of the Bureau of Reclamation and the eventual network of dams that tamed the mighty Colorado."

He dropped his foot and continued the tour, guiding Sydney toward a narrow tunnel.

"This is pretty low in spots. Watch your head."

Thankful for her borrowed hard hat, Sydney followed him into a dimly lit passageway. As the glow from the powerplant faded behind them, she entered a dark, subterranean world. The floor rose in uneven patches where concrete swirled around limestone. Water dripped from the roof of the tunnel. If she hadn't known that the reservoir was drained and not pushing millions of gallons against the tunnel, those shimmering drops would have made her distinctly nervous.

They followed the curve of the base to the canyon wall. Two spotlights were trained on the spot where concrete met sheer rock.

"See those?" Reece pointed to faint striations in the cement some feet above their heads. "Those are the stress fractures I told you about. A minor earthquake hit the area several years ago and pushed the canyon wall into the concrete. You can see the cracks more clearly from the outside now that we've blasted through the exterior wall."

Sydney eyed the hairline fractures with distinct unease. "They're not going to, uh, crack any further in the immediate future, are they?"

"The computers say no."

"What do you say, Reece?"

He hesitated, and her vivid imagination took off. She could almost feel the floor beneath her feet tremble, hear the canyon wall shriek and groan as it rubbed against concrete. Another minute and she'd be feeling millions of tons of cement tumble down on top of her.

As if sensing her growing discomfort, he took her elbow and steered her back the way they'd come. "I say we'd better go topside. You look a little green around the gills.''

Sydney had to admit the fresh air and wind whipping down the canyon soothed her jangled nerves. The sky had started spitting again, but not so hard and fast that they couldn't pause for a few moments on the walkway that led along the crest. Hard hat tipped back to catch the breeze, Reece leaned his palms on the parapet and gazed at the scurry of activity below. Sydney was content to simply hitch a hip on the wall and gaze at his profile.

It was strong and clean and almost as stubborn as the forces of nature he worked to harness. Small white squint lines showed in the tanned skin at the corners of his eyes. A faint stubble shadowed his cheeks and chin.

The artist in Sydney wanted to capture the rugged male in his natural element, silhouetted against the pewter sky and the gray sweep of his massive dam. The professional in her admired his awesome intelligence and the dedication that got him up and out to his work at 4:00 a.m. The woman in her just wanted to reach out and stroke that bristly cheek.

"What's next for you after you finish this project?" she asked curiously.

He turned then, his blue eyes lazy on her face. "I'll spend the next couple of months at our Technical Support Center in Denver, working the structural analysis on another critical repair project. My deputy will go into the field on that one, though. I haven't taken any time off in months, and I promised my brother Jake that I'd come home to help bring the cattle down from the north pastures before the snows hit.''

''Where's home?''

''A cattle ranch tucked in the foothills of the San Francisco Mountains, just north of Flagstaff. Our folks owned a spread there while I was growing up. Jake manages it now.''

''They *owned* it? Did you lose your parents, too?''

''My father died a few years ago. My mother moved off the Bar-H shortly after that.''

Keenly sensitive now to this man, Sydney wondered about the edge that had slipped into his voice. Did he still hurt with the loss of his father, as she did? Before she could probe further, he continued.

''Jake manages the spread now, along with his own place. My brothers and I try to make it home for either the spring calving or the fall roundup.'' He pushed upright, his eyes intent now as he stared down at her. ''What about you? What's next?''

''I'm looking at four to five weeks of postproduction work in my studio in L.A. Then...''

She lifted her shoulders. She had several projects in various stages of planning and development. None of them consumed her like the Weeping Woman of Chalo Canyon. And none, she realized, pulled at her as much as the need to take the next step along this magical, sensual journey of discovery with Reece.

''Maybe you could come up to the ranch,'' he suggested slowly.

Her heart thumped. ''Maybe I could.''

He moved toward her then, only a step, but Sydney's pulse skittered and spun like a videotape on Rewind. To her intense frustration, one of his men chose that moment to step out of the administration building.

"Hey, Reece! I've got the results of the flownet pressure analysis you requested of the exposed core. You wanted to go over it before we give the contractor the green light to start pouring."

"I'll be right there." The light in his eyes went from dark and intriguing to rueful. "I'm sorry."

"Don't be. I understand pressures and deadlines."

"So you do."

He swept the parking lot beside the building for Sydney's Blazer, noting Henry still ensconced in the front seat, before turning back to her.

"We'll continue this later."

She couldn't act coy if she tried. Making no effort to disguise the hunger that leaped into her veins, she rose up on tiptoe to brush a kiss across his mouth.

"Later it is."

"It'll probably be around eight-thirty," he warned. "We're going to keep going until darkness shuts us down."

"I'll be waiting."

This time, Sydney decided as she stepped into the shower just after eight that night, she intended to pull out all the stops. Reece had seen her in her boots and fatigue pants, in a towel and in nothing at all. Tonight, he was going to see a different woman, one who'd learned the art of skillful, understated makeup from one of Hollywood's masters.

Unfortunately, she hadn't brought anything elegant to wear. Something shiny and slinky and red, like the gown she'd splurged on for the Oscars. The best she could come up with after digging through all her available options were a pair of thigh-skimming flared shorts and a bright red T-shirt cut off just below her breasts, both souvenirs of a weekend at Santa Monica Beach. The shorts she'd purchased before she realized she couldn't bend over in public while wearing them. The short, midriff-baring shirt was more cool and comfortable than sexy. Taken together, however, they made a potent combination.

Humming in anticipation, she dumped the meager supply of makeup she'd brought with her into the sink and went to work. A stubby eye-liner pencil added length and depth to her eyes, careful shadows and a few, feathery strokes to the line of her brows. Lipstick, daubed lightly on her cheeks and rubbed in, doubled as blusher. Her trusty lip balm added a layer of shimmering gloss over the red she swiped on her lips.

That done, she attacked her hair with the hair drier and boar's bristle hairbrush she never traveled without. The heavy, shoulder-length mass took forever to dry, but each stroke of the brush added to its crackly shine. When it felt like raw silk in her hands, Sydney twisted it up and clamped it on top of her head with a plastic clip. Carefully she teased loose a few strands to frame her face.

Hands on hips, she surveyed the results. The overall picture didn't compare to one she'd made after four hours at one of Beverly Hills' most exclusive salons the day of the Oscars, but it would do. It would definitely do.

Humming, she padded into the bedroom. The bottle of wine she'd picked up at the Gas n' Git on the way back from the dam sat in a gray plastic bucket of ice. The man-size subs heaped with cheese and cold cuts Lula had prepared waited beside the wine.

Deciding to get a little head start, Sydney unscrewed the cap on the wine and poured a half glass. Not bad, she mused after the first sip, considering it had cost all of three ninety-nine. Wineglass in hand, she slipped the cassette from the mini-cam and slid it into the VCR that went everywhere with her.

After a long leader, Reece's face jumped out of the screen. The high-speed tape made for a slightly less vivid image than she liked, but even that small distraction didn't diminish his magnetism. Sighing with satisfaction, Sydney sank onto the bed, plumped the pillows behind her and gave herself over to the unabashed pleasure of listening to Reece explain the simple laws of physics as demonstrated by the turbines.

She had just rewound the tape and started it again when she heard a car door slam right outside. Her eyes flew to the digital clock on the nightstand. Eight twenty-seven. How like Reece to hit it almost exactly on target!

Her stomach clenching with anticipation, Sydney jumped off the bed. The soft rap of knuckles on wood had her reaching for the dead bolt and chain.

"I've got wine chilled and—"

She stopped, her throat closing in shock and dismay. Too late she realized she'd opened her door to the wrong man.

Chapter 14

"Hello, Syd."

Keeping a tight grip on the doorjamb, Sydney eyed Jamie warily. "What do you want?"

The naked bulb over the door cast her visitor's face in stark lines. Rain glinted on his hair, burnishing it to deep gold.

"I need to talk to you. Can I come in?"

"I don't think that's a good idea."

Hitching his shoulders, he shoved his hands in his pockets. A fine edge of desperation seemed to sharpen his features.

"It's important, Syd."

Her instincts shouted at her to slam the door in his face. Jamie Chavez meant nothing but trouble for her.

"Just for a moment. Please." His jaw went tight. "It's about Arlene. I just found out that she's the one who destroyed your film."

Sydney sucked in a sharp breath and stepped aside. Jamie brushed past her, looking older and more careworn than she'd ever seen him. Just to be safe she left the door open an inch or two. A single piercing scream would bring half the occupants of the motel running, not to mention Lula and Martha.

She turned to find Jamie standing in the middle of the room, his gaze snagged on the video she'd left running on the TV screen. His eyes held a cynical, knowing look when he turned them from Reece to Sydney.

"I thought you came here to document the legend of the Weeping Woman. Looks like you've found another subject that interests you."

She ignored his barbed comment. She wasn't about to discuss what was between her and Reece with this man. A quick flick of the remote killed the video playback. Tossing down the remote, she folded her arms.

"I thought *you* came here to talk about Arlene."

"I did."

"So talk."

He couldn't seem to figure out how to start. "This is hard for me. I didn't think… I didn't know…"

"How much you've hurt your wife over the years?" Sydney supplied with a lift of one brow.

"I didn't know how much she loved me," he said finally. "Or how desperate she's become."

He reached down and helped himself to a glass of wine. Sydney's lips tightened, but she bit back her automatic protest. The sooner he finished, the sooner she'd get him out of here. She had no desire to pro-

long his visit by indulging in petty arguments or re-
criminations.

Throwing back his head, Jamie tossed down the
white zinfandel like it was water. He stared at the
empty glass for a moment before continuing.

"Arlene broke down tonight. The combination of
two martinis and those damned diet pills she gobbles
like candy got to her, I guess." He shuddered. "It
wasn't a pleasant scene."

Poor baby, Sydney thought cynically. He was finally having to face up to reality.

"She poured out doubts and insecurities I didn't
even know she had." Obviously shaken, he paced
the small space between the bed and the door. "She
even told me that she's been seeing a shrink in Phoenix. All this time I thought she was going to have
her hair and nails done. She's been in therapy and
never told me."

He looked across the room, his eyes beseeching.
"I didn't know I'd done that to her, Syd. I never
realized she was so fragile."

Sydney bit back the retort that he only had to look
at his wife, really look at her, and he would have
seen how fragile she was. Reece had seen it, had
even pretended a relationship with a near stranger to
save Arlene the embarrassment of watching her husband put the make on another woman. But then,
Reece wasn't Jamie.

Thank God!

Her visitor seemed lost in contemplation of his
empty glass.

"Arlene admitted that she destroyed my film?"

Sydney prompted when it seemed as though the silence would stretch indefinitely.

He nodded, lifting his head. "She's jealous of you. Of your success and your looks. She can't forget what happened between us ten years ago."

"Well, I have. And I hope to heck you told her that you have, too."

"I tried." He blew out a long breath. "She's sorry about the videotapes, Syd. Really sorry. We want to cover any extra expenses you might have incurred as a result."

Relenting, Sydney sighed. "I don't care so much about the cost as the lost footage."

He fidgeted with his glass, then poured himself another helping. "Look, I'd appreciate it if you'd call the sheriff's office and tell them you don't want to press charges."

"Ah, now the real reason for your visit comes out." A hint of anger crept into her voice. "The proud Chavez family don't want to see one of their own charged with malicious destruction of property."

"*I* don't want to see my wife charged."

"And your father doesn't play in this, I suppose?"

"He doesn't know anything about it, or that I was coming to see you. I didn't even tell Arlene."

Suddenly she was tired of the whole mess. She couldn't believe she'd ever thought herself in love with this man. Even more to the point, she'd discovered that what she'd felt all those years ago hadn't even come close to love.

She had a pretty good idea now of what comprised that all-consuming emotion. The basic ingredients included listening to a man talk about his work in the claustrophobic confines of a narrow tunnel and thrilling to his passion for what he did. Wanting desperately to hear his low growl of laughter, to feel his hands on her body. Tingling with excitement at the thought of going home with him to a ranch tucked in the foothills of the San Francisco Mountains.

Impatient now to be rid of Jamie, she plucked the glass out of his hand and escorted him to the door.

"I'll call Martinez tomorrow and tell him I won't press charges in the matter of the destruction of the tapes. I can't say I'll feel as forgiving if it turns out Arlene engineered my accident on Canyon Rim Road."

Jamie stopped dead in his tracks. "What are you talking about?"

"Reece thinks someone may have helped that slab of limestone fall, right where the road hairpins around a curve."

"The hell he does!"

"In light of what you've told me tonight, Martinez will want to talk to Arlene about where she was the day of the accident."

High spots of color flagged Jamie's cheeks. Before Sydney could evade them, his hands whipped out and wrapped around her forearms.

"Are you saying you think my wife tried to kill you?"

"Your wife...or your father," Sydney shot back, twisting in his grip.

"You're crazy!"

"And you're starting to annoy me. Big-time. Let me go."

Instead his fingers dug deeper into her arms. His voice rose to a furious shout. "My wife wouldn't hurt a flea!"

"She did a heck of a number on my tapes!"

Incensed at the manhandling, Sydney tried to jerk free. When that didn't work, she aimed a kick at his shins. In self-defense, he hauled her up against his chest.

"Dammit, Sydney, calm down!"

"Go to hell, Chavez!"

She managed to get an arm free and aimed an awkward swing at his chin. He caught her fist just before it connected, and twisted her arm behind her back.

"For God's sake, you always were a hothead! You and your father. He had no business taking a swing at my father the way he did."

"Is that right?"

Her arm pinned against her back, her hair tumbling from its clip, Sydney could barely speak over her fury. Jamie could badmouth her all he wanted, but no one, *no one* put down her father and lived to tell about it.

"I have a lot more respect for a man who would defend his daughter than one who'd tuck his tail between his legs and scurry away at *his* father's command."

Scorn dripped from every word. The flush staining Jamie's cheeks grew brick-red. Before he could get out the hot retort that bared his teeth, however, a heartbroken cry spun his head around.

"Jamie! Oh, God, Jamie!"

He froze. His expression would have been comical in its dismay if anyone was in the mood to laugh.

"Arlene!" A hoarse denial ripped from his throat. "This isn't what it looks like."

Sebastian's outraged voice rose above the anguish coming in little, choking cries from Arlene.

"I knew it! I knew that woman would try to get her claws in you!"

The woman in question fought a groan. She couldn't believe it! Talk about déjà vu! It was ten years ago all over again.

"You ass," she hissed at Jamie. "Let me go."

"What?"

Stunned by the turn of events, he stared down at her blankly. She opened her mouth to repeat the furious order, but it got lost in a new commotion outside.

Doors slammed. Footsteps pounded. Lula's voice came screeching through the air. "We heard the shoutin'! What's going on?"

Martha added her squeaky demand to her sister's. "What are you doing in Sydney's room, Sebastian?" The footsteps skidded to a halt. "Arlene! You're here, too? And Jamie? Oh, my! Oh, my goodness!"

Enough was enough. Her face flaming, Sydney yanked free of Jamie's hold. She was damned if she was going to explain or apologize or burn with humiliation. Not again. Never again.

"You said you didn't love her!" Arlene cried. She clung to Sebastian's arm as if she couldn't support herself. "Just tonight, just an hour ago, you told me that you'd never loved her."

"I didn't." Jamie swallowed painfully, his face

now as pale as it had been red a few moments ago. "It was just a summer fling."

Sydney had found that out the hard way ten years ago. She didn't particularly enjoy having it rebroadcast for public consumption, however.

"Then what are you doing here?" Arlene sobbed. "Why are you in her room?"

Ha! That put him on the spot. Folding her arms, Sydney let Jamie find his own way out of that one.

"I came to talk to her about the videotapes."

Sebastian's aristocratic face sharpened. Shaking free of his daughter-in-law's hold, he strode into the room to stand between Sydney and his son.

"What about the tapes?"

The younger Chavez squared his chin. "I destroyed them and I—"

"You!" Sebastian's head reared back.

Arlene's sobs caught in her throat. She gaped at her husband, her eyes wide and confused. "Jamie…"

He cut her off sharply. "It was a stupid thing to do. I have no rationale, no reason."

Except the desire to protect his wife, Sydney thought. Grudgingly she recognized what Jamie himself didn't seem to. He cared enough for Arlene to want to spare her public humiliation. He certainly hadn't cared that much for Sydney ten years ago.

"I came here tonight to ask her not to press charges," he finished stiffly, his eyes cutting to Sydney as if daring her to contradict him…or bring up the business of the accident on Canyon Rim Road.

She did neither. She was heartily sick of the whole Chavez clan. She would let Deputy Martinez sort out

their assorted stories. That was his job. She had just
started to tell them so when the sound of brakes
screeching brought all heads around.

Reece!

Sydney's heart jumped with relief, with dismay,
with the almost farcical irony of the situation. Reece
had heard all the stories about her scandalous past.
His blue eyes tinged with disgust, he'd stepped in
personally to divert Jamie's attention that first night
at the café. Would he believe Chavez had come to
her room tonight just to talk, or automatically assume
the worst, as everyone else had?

Would he walk away from her, as Jamie had once
done?

No, he wouldn't walk away. Not Reece. Still, Sydney's chin tipped in anticipation of the explanations
she knew he'd demand.

Reece had spotted the crowd milling around the
door to Unit Twelve the moment he turned into the
parking lot. He was out of the Jeep and running before it had rolled to a full stop. His heart hammering,
he shouldered his way through the crowd at the door.
He didn't pull in a whole breath until he spotted Sydney, her hair tumbling down and her eyes fierce.

She looked like a mountain cat cornered by a pack
of hungry wolves. Her eyes spit green fire. Her claws
were unsheathed. She wasn't going down without a
fight.

His only thought as he walked into the room was
to get his woman away from the voracious pack. He
took in the two wineglasses, the rumpled bed, the
tears streaking Arlene's face in a single, sweeping
glance.

"Are you okay?" he asked Sydney quietly.

"Yes."

The stiff little response spoke volumes. She was writhing inside, but too damned proud to show it. Now that he knew she was safe, Reece decided the first order of business was to clear the room and give her some breathing space.

"Okay, folks. The show's over. Why don't we all call it a night."

The casual order carried an underlying note of steel. Those outside the door drifted away, murmuring. His expression almost as fierce as Sydney's, Jamie Chavez gave Reece a hard look, then walked across the room to slide an arm around his wife's waist. She collapsed against him, crying into his shoulder as he led her away.

Only Sebastian Chavez remained. Rigid. Unyielding. His black eyes cold and scornful in his proud face.

"She's a slut, Henderson. She seduced my son ten years ago and came back to Chalo Canyon to finish what she started then."

Reece rocked on the balls of his feet, his hands curling into fists. "The only reason I don't flatten you right here, right now, Chavez, is the fact that I carry forty pounds more in weight than you and thirty fewer years. I might forget those fine distinctions, however, if you don't get the hell out of here."

"She'll destroy you, too, if you let her."

Reece took a step forward. "Now, Chavez!"

Sebastian's nostrils flared. He glared at Reece for another few seconds, shot Sydney a venomous look, then spun on his heel and stalked out. Reece shut the door behind him, noting that the locks showed no signs of forced entry. Evidently Sydney had let that parade from her past into her room.

He would talk to her later about that bit of foolishness, he decided. Right now he figured she needed one thing, and one thing only. The same thing he did.

He strode back to her, dipped, and swept her up in his arms. The single chair in the room looked too rickety to hold them both, but Reece decided to chance it.

Sydney lay stiff against his chest for several long moments. He could feel her trembling. Subduing his seething fury at the Chavezes for subjecting her to this public debacle, he held her loose against his chest.

Finally she twisted upright in his lap. "Don't you want to know what happened?"

"I can pretty well figure it out."

Her chin came up. A militant sparkle lit her eyes. She was still feeling the sting of Sebastian's parting shot, Reece guessed.

"Just what have you figured out?"

"Jamie came knocking on your door and talked his way inside."

"And?"

The belligerence in her tone tugged at Reece's heart. She'd gone down this road once before.

"And," he said calmly, "Chavez Jr. proceeded to make a total ass of himself. You were in the process of showing him out when his wife and father and everyone else in town arrived on the scene."

She stared at him, waiting for him to continue. When he didn't, her brows snapped together.

"That's it? That's what you think happened?"

"I don't think, Sydney. I know."

"How?"

He smiled at the blunt demand. A week ago, even a few days ago, he might have asked himself the same question. He'd heard all the stories about her. Had formed a less-than-flattering picture of her in his mind before he'd even met her. Since then he'd gained a deeper insight into this vital, vibrant woman. He'd seen her single-minded dedication to her work, her lively curiosity about anything and everything, even his dam. He'd laughed with her, loved with her. He couldn't imagine how he'd believed, even for a moment, the stories that painted her as the cold-hearted other woman.

Sliding fingers into her tumbled hair, he cradled her face in his palms. "I know that's what happened, because I know you."

Sydney went into the kiss stunned by his simple declaration. She came out of it aching with a love that started deep in her chest and spread at warp speed to every finger, every toe.

It was several breathless moments before she remembered Jamie's reason for knocking on her door. She struggled upright in Reece's lap once more.

"Jamie came to town tonight to tell me that Arlene slashed my videotapes."

"He ratted on his wife?" Reece's lip curled. "Nice guy."

Much as it went against the grain to defend the man, Sydney had to admit the truth. "No, he didn't come to rat on her, only to ask me to drop the charges.''

The last of her old resentments slipped away as she related how Jamie had leaped to Arlene's defense. He loved her, even if he didn't know the extent of that love. He'd always loved her. Sydney could only blame her own foolish infatuation on the fact that she hadn't recognized that fact any more than Jamie had.

''So are you?'' Reece asked. ''Going to drop the charges?'' he added when she looked at him blankly.

Smiling, she shook off the past forever. ''Of course. I don't want to hurt Arlene. I never did.''

Looping her arms around his neck, she brushed his mouth with hers. With the touch came a gradual awareness. She *didn't* want to hurt Arlene. She didn't want to hurt anyone. She drew back, her eyes filling with regret.

''Maybe Sebastian was right.''

Reece's palm slid around her nape. His thumb tipped her chin. ''Not hardly.''

The snarl warmed Sydney's heart.

''I didn't come back here for revenge or intending to destroy Jamie's marriage, but I've certainly added to the stresses. If my presence pushed Arlene to such destructive, vengeful acts, I think— No, I know. I need to go back to L.A. and leave them in peace.''

He didn't say anything.

''I'll pack up tomorrow, Reece.''

''What about your documentary?''

She let out a long gust of breath. ''I'll use what footage I have and exercise my creativity to fill in where I have to.''

Reece didn't even try to dissuade her. After seeing the look in Sebastian's eyes, his gut told him that the old man's hatred went far deeper than Arlene's. Or maybe it was fear. Whatever drove him, Reece wanted Sydney out of the line of fire.

He knew what leaving would cost her, however, and how much this documentary meant to her. The fact that she'd pack up before she completed her shoot opened a crack in his heart.

"I'll come get you in L.A.," he said with a smile that promised everything he didn't have the words to express, "and take you home to meet my brothers."

"Are they as tough as you?"

"Tougher."

"As big?"

"Bigger."

She traced a fingertip along his jaw. "As handsome?"

"No, ma'am," he said without a blink. "They're ugly as sin and twice as mean. I'm the best of the lot."

Laughing, she dropped a kiss on his mouth.

"I'll remember that."

Chapter 15

Sydney said goodbye to Reece in the predawn darkness. The farewells took longer than either of them anticipated, particularly since they involved an unexpected detour back to bed.

Finally Reece groaned and pulled himself out of her arms. "I'll see you in L.A. within a week. Two, at most. If the repair work takes longer than anticipated, I'll fly in for a night at least."

"Is that a promise?"

"That, sweetheart, is a promise."

Every nerve in Sydney's body hummed with pleasure at the look in his eyes. He was, she now knew, a man of his word. This time she wasn't leaving an aching heart behind when she left Chalo Canyon.

She was still languid with pleasure when she rolled out of bed a few hours later, showered and began to pack her things. She stepped outside to a spitting rain and went down to the café for coffee and a quick breakfast.

Henry Three Pines was waiting for her, his gnarled hands folded around a mug of Lula's dark, steaming brew.

"We will not need the snakes to ask the kachinas for much rain this year," he observed when she joined him.

"Not this year," she agreed.

Someday, Sydney thought, she should document the famous Hopi snake dance that took place each summer after eight days of secret rituals. But she'd only shoot from a distance. She had no desire to get in close to the dancers who snatched up live rattlesnakes and carried them around in their mouths before releasing them to carry the tribe's pleas for rain to the gods.

She and Henry sat in companionable silence for a few moments, each contemplating the rain outside, before Sydney sighed.

"I'm going home today."

"So I have heard. I will send my grandsons down into the canyon this morning to remove the ladders and equipment you rented."

"Thank you."

His calm gaze settled on her face. "It's a wise decision, Little Squirrel. You have found what you sought when you came back here."

A blush started at her neck and worked its way to her cheeks. Under the brim of his brown felt hat, Henry's weathered face folded into a million wrinkles.

"I meant the peace your spirit needed," he said

with a grin. "But it is good that you found Reece, also." His hand closed over hers. "Your father would be happy for you."

"I think so, too."

Sydney thought about Henry's words as she settled her bill and made her farewells to Lula and Martha. Despite the fact that she had gaping holes in her documentary and would have to scramble to fill them with stock footage, she was leaving Chalo Canyon feeling far more serenity than when she'd arrived.

Serenity…and a simmering, sizzling joy.

As if to echo her mood, the sun broke through the clouds unexpectedly just as she hit the two-lane road that led out of town. The Blazer hummed along for another few miles, soaking up the hazy sunshine. As it approached a Y in the road, Sydney eased up on the accelerator.

She could cut right and take the private road through Sebastian's land to save herself twenty miles, or detour around his property as she'd done for the past ten days. The temptation to thumb her nose at him and drive across his land tugged at her, but she swung left and took the longer route. The last thing she wanted was another encounter with any of the Chavez clan.

A few miles down the road, she approached the State Road that ran north and south. South would take her to Phoenix and the airport. North…north would take her to the canyon rim and the pull-off where she and her crew had parked their vehicles before trekking down into the canyon.

The Blazer slowed to a stop. Crossing her hands

over the wheel, Sydney contemplated the black-topped road. The sun still shone through the gray clouds, but the light was getting weaker by the moment. She chewed on her lower lip, aching for one last shot at the ruins. She had time. Her flight to L.A. didn't take off for another four hours.

Digging in her purse, she pulled out her cell phone and punched in the number for Reece's. She'd just about given up hope that he'd answer when his voice snapped.

"Henderson."

She could barely hear him over the roar of machinery in the background. He must be down at the base of the dam, near that monster crane.

"Reece, it's Sydney. I'm on my way to the airport."

"Drive safe. Let me know when you get there."

"I will. Listen, I'm only a few miles from the path that leads into the canyon. I'm going down for one more shot while this light holds."

"What?" He had to yell over the ear-splitting noise in the background.

"I'm going to make a brief stop at the ruins."

"That's not a good idea!"

"Everyone thinks I've left town. It's safe."

"No, it's not. Those clouds…" He broke off, cursing as gears shrieked like the demons of hell. "Those clouds to the north have dumped a lot of rain on the mesas. Our recorders haven't registered any measurable threat of flooding yet, but— What? Okay, okay," he shouted in an aside. "I'll be right there."

"I'll only stay a few minutes," she assured him when she had his attention again. "Just enough for some shots of the tower where the Weeping Woman was imprisoned. I won't get the interiors I need, but at least I'll have a few exteriors focused exclusively on the tower and the window she supposedly jumped from. I'll be in and out of the canyon in an hour and a half.''

"All right," he conceded with heavy reluctance. "Just keep your phone handy and hotfoot it out of there immediately if I call and tell you to."

"I will."

Eager for a chance to showcase the tower in a last, dramatic sequence, Sydney grabbed the hard-sided case that held the minicam and its assorted lenses, locked the car and stuffed the keys in one of her many pockets. The cell phone went in another. Thank goodness she'd opted for the comfort of her baggy pants and sneakers for the return trip to L.A.! Slinging the strap of the camera case over her shoulder, she hurried down the path. She'd made the trek in and out of the canyon often enough by now to know every bump and turn and slide of rocks by heart.

Hurrying, she reached river level within ten minutes, the ruins in another fifteen. Sweaty from exertion and the muggy dampness of the impending rain, she gave a silent prayer of thanks when the wind started to pick up. The frisky breeze lifted the damp hair off her neck and tossed stray tendrils at will. Within moments, she had the viewfinder to her eye and was trying to find just the right angles.

Intent on her task, Sydney moved sideways along the river bank, shooting a series of shorts, longs and wide angles that focused on the shadowy window at the top of the square tower. She wished to heck she could climb up to the cave and get inside the Weeping Woman's supposed prison, but Henry's grandsons had already picked up the ladders, and there was no way Sydney was going to attempt those shallow handholds dug into the cliff face.

She finished one thirty-minute Betacam tape, dropped it in her pocket and was just getting ready to insert another when the wind began to whistle down the canyon in earnest. Rising. Falling. A soughing cry.

Aiiiii. Eee-aiiiii.

One by one, the hair on the back of Sydney's neck lifted. It sounded just like the tiny, hollow-cheeked retired schoolteacher turned eccentric, Laura Brent, calling to her. Sydney had already decided to pack it in when the rumble of thunder brought her head up with a jerk. Even as she watched, billowing clouds rolled across the sun. The sky darkened instantly to an angry gray.

"Whoa! Time to make tracks, girl!"

Where there was thunder, lightning was sure to follow. Or was it the other way around? In either case, she had no desire to get zapped by those two zillion amps Reece had talked about.

He confirmed her decision when he called a moment later.

"Get out of there!" he barked. "Now! The rain's coming down in sheets north of here."

"I'm on my way."

"Call me as soon as you're on the path up to the rim."

"I will."

She was fitting the minicam into its case when another sound carried over the eerie cry of the wind. A faint slide of rock on rock. A heavy tread. She spun around and went rigid with shock.

Sebastian moved toward her. Slowly. Steadily. His silver hair whipped in the wind, but the evil-looking automatic pistol in his hand didn't waver. The hatred in his black eyes caught Sydney by the throat.

"I knew you were lying about leaving Chalo Canyon."

She didn't bother to ask how he knew about her abrupt departure. Gossip traveled at the speed of light in a small town. Besides, she wasn't sure she could speak around the baseball-size lump in her throat.

"Your kind always lies."

"No, it's true. I'm leaving. Today. Right now, if you'll just…"

She swallowed her disjointed words and stumbled back a pace as he came nearer. Her fingers gripped the strap of the camera case as if it were a lifeline to reality, sanity. Safety.

"Didn't you see my car? The Blazer?" she asked desperately. "It's all packed."

"I saw it. That's how I knew you had come down into the canyon."

"How could you miss the suitcases and the equipment in the back? I'm leaving Chalo Canyon, Sebastian. I swear, I'm leaving."

He smiled then, a slight rearrangement of his facial muscles that churned Sydney's mounting terror into bile.

"That's what Marianne said."

"Who?"

"My wife. She was a slut, like you. The only thing she did right in our short marriage was give birth to Jamie." His smile slipped into a fury that was all the more frightening for being so cold, so implacable. "Even then, she taunted me, tried to tell me he wasn't my son."

With a calm detachment that horrified Sydney, he pulled back the automatic's slide and cocked it. Hands out, camera case dangling from one wrist, she made a desperate attempt to reason with the man.

"Sebastian! Wait! I didn't come back to Chalo Canyon to hurt you or your son, only to make a documentary. You have to believe me!"

"I believe you," he said grimly. "I've believed you all along."

"Then what…why…?"

"Why do I have to kill you? Because I don't want that film made."

Sydney's hair whipped in her face, stinging her cheeks. She didn't dare reach up to clear it for fear the movement would trigger a reaction from the man only a few yards from her.

"My documentary won't dishonor the Anasazi! If anything, it might stir interest in the Ancient Ones."

"You fool! Haven't you realized that's exactly what I fear? Your cursed movie will bring a horde of archeologists and anthropologists down on the ruins every time the reservoir drains. Maybe even scuba divers during the years the village is underwater, poking around in the ruins, trying to find artifacts."

"But…"

Suddenly his eyes blazed. "Don't you understand?

I don't want them up there! I didn't want you up there, disturbing old ghosts!''

"You mean the Weeping Woman? But that's just a legend."

The smile came back, so cold, so terrifying, that Sydney's heart froze.

"Is it?"

Her mind went blank for several seconds. Absolutely, totally, completely blank. Then the bits of gossip mixed with local lore she'd picked up exploded into her thoughts, ripping through her imagination like shrapnel.

"Oh, my God! She's up there, isn't she? Your wife? Lula said…" Frantic, Sydney tried to recall the on-camera interview with the Jenkins sisters. "She said she first heard the legend of the Weeping Woman about thirty years ago. From you…not long after your wife disappeared."

She wet her lips, her horror mounting as she fit the pieces of the puzzle together. "The story shook Lula so much she never trekked down into the canyon again. That's what you intended, isn't it? That's why you made up the tale about the Weeping Woman? To scare people away from the ruins."

"I didn't make it all up. I'd heard a similar tale as a child and simply embellished it."

His lip curled. The face Sydney had always thought of as aristocratic became a twisted mask.

"Appropriate, don't you think? Marianne planned to leave me for someone else. I never learned who. When she threatened to take Jamie away with her, I knew I could never let her leave Chalo Canyon alive.

She became the Weeping Woman, crying for her lost love.''

''Sebastian…''

''She's been buried under the rubble in that tower for more than thirty years. She would have slept for eternity if you hadn't decided to poke around in the ruins and make your damned—''

Without warning, the skies split. Lightning cracked. Instinctively Sebastian hunched his shoulders and whipped his head around for a second to see where it hit. Only for a second.

Sydney knew that second was all she'd get. In an explosive burst of fear and adrenaline, she fisted her hand around the camera case strap and swung with every ounce of strength she possessed.

The hard-sided case hit Sebastian's arm with a glancing blow, knocking it in a wild arc. The automatic flew out of his hand and clattered against stone. Before he could recover his balance, she followed up with another, even more vicious swing. This one slammed into his right temple. He grunted, then crumpled to the earth.

Her blood roaring in her ears, Sydney stood over him. Panting, gasping, swimming in adrenaline, she hefted the case again, held it high above her head, her arms shaking with the strain, until she felt sure he wasn't feigning.

He was out cold.

For how long, she couldn't guess. And she sure didn't intend to stick around to find out. Scrambling in the direction the gun had flown, she searched desperately for a sight of its gleaming blue steel. She didn't want to leave it behind for him to find if and

when he came to and started after her. She'd taken
only a single step when her cell phone shrilled, almost stopping her heart.

Sucking in air, she kept a wary eye on Sebastian,
dug in her pockets for the phone and tried to find the
damned automatic, all at the same time. Finally she
fumbled the phone free and flipped it up.

"Sydney!" Reece roared. "Where are you?"

"At the ruins. Sebas—"

"I told you to get out of there!"

"I was on my way, but—"

"You don't have time to make it to the path.
You'll have to go up the cliff face! Now!"

She shot an incredulous look at the handholds
carved into the rock. "Are you crazy?"

"Listen to me. I just got a call from the water-
monitoring station twenty miles north of here. An
arroyo that used to drain into the west mesa crumbled
and changed course. Its spill is now pouring into the
Chalo. There's a wall of water and mud eight feet
high roaring down the canyon. I've called in a chopper for you, but—"

She didn't like the sound of that "but." She didn't
like the sound of any of this!

"I'll take the Jeep and get to you as fast as I can.
Just get up that cliff face!"

"Reece, Sebastian's here." She wrapped both
hands around the phone, her hair whipping wildly.
"He tried to shoot me. I knocked him out."

"Oh, God!" His breath exploded in her ear. "I've
got a rope in the Jeep. I'll come down for Sebastian
when I get there. Start climbing, Sydney. Now!"

Abandoning all thoughts of the gun, she ran for

the cliff. Halfway there, she stumbled to a halt. She swung around, panting, to stare at Sebastian's unmoving form. She couldn't just leave the bastard there to drown. Could she?

Cursing a blue streak at her own idiocy, Sydney raced back to the comatose man and grabbed his arm. Grunting, panting, she dragged him toward the cliff. She didn't have the faintest idea how she'd get him up the sheer rock face.

She'd figure that out when she got there.

Down canyon, Reece slammed the phone shut and raced along the dam's thick, curving base. He'd already activated the emergency flood-warning-alert system, but the responsibility for the safety of the men working on-site as well as the residents of the towns downriver sat on his shoulders like a ton of concrete. He had only seconds to think, to analyze the situation, only moments to decide what to do.

In a flash flood situation like this, the correct procedure was to close the spillgates and trap the rushing water behind the dam. The massive structure would contain it, keep it from rushing on and ravaging the towns downriver. The dam had been constructed all those years ago for just that purpose.

In this case, however, the rampaging floodwater would hit an exposed core, one already weakened by stress fractures. The whole dam could give under the sudden, added force.

And it would! Reece knew it with everything in him. Despite the computer analyses, despite X-rays and geophysical in-situ testing, Reece knew the base wouldn't hold without some kind of reinforcement.

Worry and fear for Sydney gnawing at his gut, he raced for the two men conferring at the repair site.

"Call up top," he ordered his deputy. "Tell them to close the floodgates. Then I want the dam cleared of all personnel."

His second in command nodded, but his eyes mirrored Reece's own worry. "If we've got as much water coming at us as they said, this baby won't take the added stress."

"She'll have to."

The engineer threw a wrenching look at the crater blasted out of the curving base. "Not with her core exposed like that."

"We're not going to leave it exposed." He shot an order at the contractor. "I want your crane operator to ram his machine up against the hole. Let it take the force of the water, act as a kind of a plug."

"That piece of equipment cost fifteen million dollars!"

"I'll take full responsibility." His lips stretched in a grim smile. "If this doesn't work and the entire dam comes down on top of the crane, they can deduct the cost of a replacement from my paycheck."

"Dammit, Reece...!"

"You got a better idea?"

The contractor hesitated, shook his head.

"Then do it!" Already on the run, he shouted again for his deputy to clear the dam.

"Where are you going?"

"There are people trapped up canyon. I've got to get to them."

He had to get to Sydney!

Flinging himself inside the tiny elevator, he

stabbed at the buttons. Every verse of the Bible his mother had drummed into her five unruly sons ran through his heart during the agonizingly slow ride to the top. The moment he shoved open the elevator door, the sound of a helicopter coming in low and fast assaulted his ears.

The bird set down in the parking lot, its maroon-and-silver logo glistening in the rain. Reece ducked under the whirring blades, yanked open the passenger door and climbed aboard.

"I heard you called for a rescue chopper," Jamie shouted over the scream of the rotor. "I came to help."

"Let's go!"

They lifted off mere seconds later. For the duration of the short ride, Reece listened to the reports from upriver, confirmed that the crane was in place and his men had cleared the dam, and prayed that Sydney had managed to climb up the cliff face.

Rain pelted down, knifing into her flesh. Panting, Sydney shook her hair out of her eyes and tried to gauge the distance to the cliff. Another ten yards. Maybe fifteen.

Her breath stabbed at her lungs. Her knees and back were bent with the strain of dragging Sebastian's dead weight. She had him almost to the foot of the cliff when he groaned.

"Sebastian!" She dropped to her knees, shook his shoulders. "Sebastian, wake up!"

He moaned again and put a shaking hand to his temple.

"You've got to climb up to the ruins! Reece says there's a flash flood…"

His eyes opened. He stared at her dully.

"Listen to me!" She shouted over the screaming wind. "We've got to climb up to the ruins. Reece says there's a flash flood up canyon. It's coming right at us!"

He staggered to his feet and looked around wildly, as if trying to remember where he was. When his glance came back to her, his face twisted.

"I can't let you leave Chalo Canyon alive, you witch. I can't let you take my son."

Still woozy, still off balance from the blow, he lunged for her. Sydney danced away from him easily. Desperate, she tried to think past the fear roaring in her ears of some way to reach him, to make him understand…

Suddenly, she realized that the roar in her ears wasn't fear. She threw a terrified glance up canyon. It sounded like a freight train was tearing right at them.

"Sebastian!"

All around them the roar rose to a deafening pitch. For a moment she stared into eyes blinded by hate. Then Sebastian lurched away.

"I'll find my gun. I'll end this now. You won't leave. You won't take my son away."

Sobbing, shaking with terror, Sydney stuck her toe into an indentation carved out of the rock. Her scrabbling right hand found a hole just above her head. Her left, another a little higher up. She pulled herself up, scraped her foot across the rock until she found purchase, pulled again.

She didn't dare look up to measure the distance to the cave for fear she'd overbalance and fall backward. Nor could she look down to see if Sebastian was climbing the cliff below her or still searching for his damned gun. Her skin crawled with the fear that he would find it. She could almost feel the bullets slamming into her body.

Sweating, straining, deafened by the howling wind and nerve-shattering roar, she crabbed up the cliff face.

She was halfway to the cave when a wall of muddy water came bursting around the canyon's bend. It crashed toward her, under her, slapping upward, sucking at her feet, her legs. Sydney clung to the wall, her face pressed into stone, her nails clawing at rock.

Then, as fast as it had come, the crest passed. The angry water dropped a foot, a yard, raged on below her. Her fingers numb, her shoulder and calf muscles on fire, she tried to find the strength for the rest of the climb. Only then did she hear Reece's voice amplified a thousand times over, bouncing off the canyon walls.

"Grab the harness! Sydney, behind you! Grab the harness!"

Chapter 16

For the rest of her life, Sydney would remember the day the Chalo raged through the canyon, bringing with it moments of terrifying fear and blinding joy.

One of the worst moments came just after Reece hauled her aboard the chopper. As soon as she caught her breath, she shouted over the noise of the blades to Jamie.

"Your father's down there!"

He took his eyes from the controls long enough for her to see the wrenching anguish in his eyes.

"Reece said he came after you. Tried to shoot you."

She nodded, her throat closing at his pain.

"I did this to him."

The words tore out of Jamie's throat as he stared through the rain-splattered windshield, his arms and legs automatically working the chopper's controls.

"I worried him sick about Arlene and me. I made him think that you, that I—"

"No! It wasn't you." Leaning past Reece, Sydney grabbed his shoulder. "It wasn't you. I'll tell you everything later...when we find him." Her fingers dug into his wet shirt. "He may still be alive. We may find him."

Even as she shouted the encouragement, Reece shook his head. Sebastian's son put what Reece didn't say into flat, hard words.

"He couldn't have survived that." His jaw locked. "And I can't search for his body now. We've got to get back to the dam, see if it's going to hold. If not, my first, my only priority is to evacuate the ranch, make sure Arlene is safe."

The dam! Sydney clutched the edges of the thin, silver solar blanket Reece had wrapped around her. Her frightened eyes sought his.

"Those stress fractures? The ones you were so worried about? They're taking the brunt of the river?"

Incredibly, he flashed her a grin. It was weak and strained around the edges, but it was definitely a grin.

"With the help of a fifteen-million-dollar crane."

Gulping, she sank back on the helo's side seat. Her all-too-vivid imagination kicked into high gear. She could see the dam crumbling, hear the tearing groan of concrete giving way. After her own experience in the canyon, she had no difficulty imagining the terror of the residents of the town when the floodwaters came roaring down on them.

She didn't take a whole breath until the chopper swooped around a bend of the canyon and the Chalo

River Dam rose ahead of them. Proud, curved, glistening in the rain, it had caught the floodwaters and thrown them back.

Muddy water churned angrily, slapped up the dam's spine, tearing down what remained of the scaffolding. Only the arm of a massive crane poked out of the swirling mass.

Fascinated, horrified, wishing with all her heart she had a camera to record this awesome spectacle, Sydney jumped out of the helo right behind Reece when they touched down in the parking lot. They joined the cluster of men at the canyon's edge, watching, waiting.

Finally the water found its level. The churning subsided. A profound stillness descended.

After what seemed like a lifetime, Reece broke the silence. "All right. The river's settling. We'll take the spillgates to quarter-open and release the floodwaters at forty cubic feet per second. That should mitigate the impact downriver."

Forty cubic feet sounded like a whole lot to Sydney, but from the grunts of agreement that rose all around her, she suspected it would do the trick. The fierce expression in Reece's eyes when he turned to her confirmed her suspicions.

"We did it! We beat the river."

Smiling, she shook her head. "You did it."

"Stay here, okay? Don't go near the ramparts until we bring the floodwaters down and I give the all clear." A glint of laughter lightened the intensity of his blue eyes. "I don't think my heart could take having to haul you out of any more trees or floods."

"I don't think mine could, either!"

He kissed her, hard and fast and very thoroughly, then strode off to join his men.

Sighing, Sydney watched him disappear into the administration building. She would have preferred to go with him, to get a glimpse of what came next. She needed the visual to flesh out the idea for the documentary that had taken shape in her head.

She'd use stock footage from the thirties and forties. Show the construction of the early dams like Hoover and Hungry Horse up in Montana. Document their repairs over the years. Highlight the efforts of today's engineers to adapt yesterday's structures to new technology, new environmental standards. The theme would be man working with nature, struggling to find that perfect balance between...

The sight of Jamie Chavez standing alone beside his chopper shut down her rush of creative enthusiasm like a fist falling on steel. As she watched, he turned to climb back into the helo.

He was going to look for his father. She saw it in his bleak face and stiff, jerky movements.

Despite the terror Sebastian had put her through, she understood his son's pain. She'd gone through the same, searing loss herself just a few months ago. She didn't move, didn't try to stop him. There'd be time enough later to tell him what happened down at the ruins, tell him as well about his mother.

That time came late that evening.

Haggard and slump-shouldered, Jamie walked into the Lone Eagle Café. Arlene was at his side. She spotted Sydney and Reece first.

Across tables littered with the remains of the steak

and beans Reece's ravenous crew had wolfed down, the two women stared at each other. Without saying a word, Arlene left her husband's side and crossed the room.

Reece rose at her approach. He kept silent, recognizing that this was between the two of them.

"I'm sorry," Arlene said hoarsely. "About your videotapes. About—" she lifted a hand so thin the veins stood out, let it drop "—about everything."

Sydney nodded.

"The search-and-rescue crew found Sebastian's body."

"We heard."

Arlene swallowed painfully. "Jamie's devastated, but he has to— He wants to—"

"I have to know," her husband finished, coming to stand behind his wife.

Once more Sydney nodded. "We can go to Reece's room and talk there."

"This is fine," Jamie said with a twist of his lips. "There are no secrets in a small town. You know that."

"Maybe not," Lula put in, huffing out from behind the counter, "but some matters are best left between friends and family."

Plunking mugs of coffee down on the table for Arlene and Jamie, she proceeded to clear the café of everyone but the four people at the table. The door slammed behind her.

With a gesture of weary courtesy, Jamie pulled a chair out for his wife. He sank down in the one next to her.

Sydney had spent most of the afternoon trying to

decide how to tell him about his father's desperation. *Whether* to tell him. Sebastian was dead. Would it help his son to know that the father he loved had killed his mother?

Sydney had spent her adult years recording the truth as seen through a camera. As a documentarian, she knew that truth was never what it seemed. But this story wasn't hers to edit or shape. She knew she had to tell Jamie those harsh, bare facts and let him shape his own truth.

Swallowing, she related the story of the Weeping Woman of Chalo Canyon.

Three days later, Joe Martinez and two other deputies, assisted by a forensics specialist and an archeologist from the University of Arizona uncovered a set of bones buried beneath the rubble in the square tower. The archeologist confirmed that skeletal remains belonged to a female. The forensics specialist identified what looked like a bullet hole in her skull.

Epilogue

Sydney sat bathed in moonlight on a limestone outcropping, her arms wrapped around her knees, her gaze on the ruins across the canyon. A camera mounted on a tripod whirred beside her.

After four long months, the reservoir was slowly rising. After the damage caused by the flood and the extra reinforcement Reece had insisted on, repairs to the dam had taken longer than originally planned. Now they were done, and the water was once again rising up the canyon walls. She couldn't see its movement, couldn't measure its exact progress, but the dark waves lapped at the floor of the cave.

Soon the magical, mystical village she'd first seen as a child would sink into another long sleep. The ruins wouldn't see sunlight for ten years...more than ten years, if Reece's modified repairs proved as cost effective as he predicted.

His job here was done. Hers, too, once the village slipped beneath the waters and disappeared.

Sydney had spent the past three months editing her work, adding structure and definition to the raw footage, inserting titles and graphics, recording narration and music…in effect, sculpting her story. The rough cut had thrilled her. The fine cut would come as soon as she added the ending.

This ending.

Shivering with mingled regret and anticipation, Sydney leaned back against the solid chest behind her. Reece's arms came around her.

"Cold?"

"No. Just…sad that it's almost over. And eager to get on to the next project."

"The next project being our wedding, or your new documentary?"

Laughing, she twisted in his arms. "Our wedding. Definitely our wedding. Your brothers have threatened me with all kinds of dire retribution if I don't make an honest man out of you."

A grin tugged at Reece's lips. "You sure you want to get married on the ranch? We could sneak off for a Vegas quickie."

"No way!"

Sydney had already visited the sprawling spread Reece still thought of as home. It had been a flying trip, one day up and one day back, since she was still rushing to make her deadline. In her nervousness at meeting his mother, four brothers and two sisters-in-law, Sydney hadn't taken a camera with her. She'd regretted the omission as soon as she saw the Bar-H and the men it had bred.

She couldn't wait to go back and capture the grandeur of the San Franciscos against the blue sky...not to mention the grandeur of the *Henderson Hunks,* as the latest addition to the family had privately dubbed them.

Molly Duncan Henderson, recently married to Reece's youngest brother, Sam, had confided to Sydney that the Henderson brothers still overwhelmed her. Individually they could charm the fillings out of a girl's teeth. Collectively, they made for a powerful family. One that had welcomed Sydney with laughter and a readiness to love.

The aching sense of loss she felt at her father's death had eased up there, surrounded by Reece's family. She wanted them all at her wedding. Every one of them.

"You don't know what you're letting yourself in for," her soon-to-be groom warned when she told him so.

"Funny, that's what every one of your brothers said. Marsh, in particular, had some interesting stories to tell about you."

"Ha!" Reece unfolded his long length and rose, then lifted Sydney off the slab of limestone. "Marsh is a cynical cop who thinks every male is a potential criminal. Don't listen to him."

"What does he think about every female?"

The teasing light in Reece's eyes dimmed. "He got hurt a while back. He's still hurting."

Sydney started to ask him how, but it occurred to her that maybe Reece really didn't want to get married at the Bar-H. Maybe he, too, still carried painful memories.

After one long, particularly satisfying bout of love-making, they'd lain in each other's arms, talking about where they'd live between their respective travels, about dams and documentaries, about her father...and his.

The story had come out slowly, bit by agonizing bit. In a tight voice, Reece had shared with her what he'd never shared with his brothers. She'd held her breath while he described that awful night he'd listened to his mother sob, walked her up and down the living room, felt his faith in his father crumble into dust.

Maybe...maybe he didn't want to go back to the Bar-H and celebrate their marriage in the shadow of his mother's unhappiness. Rising up on tiptoe, Sydney cupped his face with both hands.

"What about you, Reece? Are you still hurting? Will it pain you to share our vows in the place where your parents' marriage fell apart?"

"No," he said simply. "It's home. It always will be home." A glint of laughter crept into his eyes. "Especially if I end up having to pay for the damage to that crane. We won't be able to afford anything else."

Sydney huffed with indignation, as he'd known she would. She'd been bristling ever since he explained that a report of survey, to document the damage to the crane, had to be processed before he was cleared of all liability.

"*No one* in any bureaucracy in any country in the world would charge you for that. You saved a whole town, for Pete's sake!"

He tried to look humble, but laughter kept tickling

the back of his throat. She looked so fierce, so ready to take on all comers.

"Well, I wouldn't go that far."

"I would!" She flung her arms around his neck. "You saved me, too, Reece."

"Several times," he agreed dryly.

He still shuddered every time she drove off in a car, her mind going a thousand miles a minute, her thoughts on the great visuals out the window instead of the road.

"You're still saving me," she murmured, dragging his mouth down to hers. "You save me every time you do this. And this. And—"

"Sydney…"

Groaning, he sank to his knees.

She came down with him, love splintering through her at the magical touch of his hands, his mouth. Whatever came, wherever his work and her films took them, they would always, always have this.

Behind them, the camera whirred. Across the canyon, the ruins sank slowly under the water and settled into sleep once more. A light breeze played across the surface of the water, carrying with it a sound that could have been a soft, gentle, smiling sigh.

* * * * *

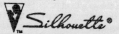

If you enjoyed what you just read,
then we've got an offer you can't resist!

Take 2 bestselling love stories FREE!

Plus get a FREE surprise gift!

THE FORTUNES OF TEXAS

This **BRAND-NEW** program includes 12 incredible stories about a wealthy Texas family rocked by scandal and embedded in mystery.

It is based on the tremendously successful *Fortune's Children* continuity.

Membership in this family has its privileges...and its price.

But what a fortune can't buy, a true-bred Texas love is sure to bring!

This exciting program will start in September 1999!

Available at your favorite retail outlet.

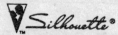

INTIMATE MOMENTS®

Silhouette®
and

DOREEN ROBERTS

invite you to the wonderful world of

RODEO MEN

A secret father, a passionate protector,
a make-believe groom—these cowboys are
husbands waiting to happen....

HOME IS WHERE THE COWBOY IS
IM #909, February 1999

A FOREVER KIND OF COWBOY
IM #927, May 1999

THE MAVERICK'S BRIDE
IM #945, August 1999

Don't miss a single one!

Available at your favorite retail outlet.

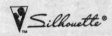

Silhouette®

**The combination of physical attraction
and danger can be explosive!**

Coming in July 1999
three steamy romances together in one book

HOT PURSUIT

by bestselling authors

JOAN JOHNSTON

ANNE STUART

MALLORY RUSH

Joan Johnston—A WOLF IN SHEEP'S CLOTHING
The Hazards and the Alistairs had been feuding for generations, so
when Harriet Alistair laid claim to her great-uncle's ranch, Nathan
Hazard was at his ornery worst. But then he saw her and figured it
was time to turn on the charm, forgive, forget…and seduce?

Anne Stuart—THE SOLDIER & THE BABY
What could possibly bring together a hard-living, bare-chested
soldier and a devout novice? At first, it was an innocent baby…and
then it was a passion hotter than the simmering jungle they had to
escape from.

Mallory Rush—LOVE SLAVE
Rand Slick hired Rachel Tinsdale to infiltrate the dark business of
white slavery. It was a risky assignment, Rachel knew. But even more
dangerous was her aching desire for her sexy, shadowy client….

Available at your favorite retail outlet.

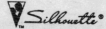

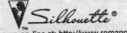

*This August 1999, the legend
continues in Jacobsville*

DIANA PALMER

LOVE WITH A
LONG, TALL TEXAN

A trio of brand-new short stories featuring
three irresistible Long, Tall Texans

GUY FENTON, LUKE CRAIG
and CHRISTOPHER DEVERELL...

This August 1999, Silhouette brings readers an
extra-special collection for Diana Palmer's legions
of fans. Diana spins three unforgettable stories of
love—Texas-style! Featuring the men you can't get
enough of from the wonderful town of Jacobsville,
this collection is a treasure for all fans!

*They grow 'em tall in the saddle in Jacobsville—and
they're the best-looking, sweetest-talking men to be
found in the entire Lone Star state. They are proud,
hardworking men of steel and it will take
the perfect woman to melt their hearts!*

**Don't miss this collection of original
Long, Tall Texans stories...available in
August 1999 at your favorite retail outlet.**

 *Silhouette* ®

THE MACGREGORS OF OLD...

#1 *New York Times* bestselling author

NORA ROBERTS

has won readers' hearts with her enormously popular MacGregor family saga. Now read about the MacGregors' proud and passionate Scottish forebears in this romantic, tempestuous tale set against the bloody background of the historic battle of Culloden.

Coming in July 1999

REBELLION

One look at the ravishing red-haired beauty and Brigham Langston was captivated. But though Serena MacGregor had the face of an angel, she was a wildcat who spurned his advances with a rapier-sharp tongue. To hot-tempered Serena, Brigham was just another Englishman to be despised. But in the arms of the dashing and dangerous English lord, the proud Scottish beauty felt her hatred melting with the heat of their passion.

Available at your favorite retail outlet.

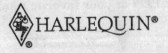

HARLEQUIN®